ABOUT THAT KISS

HARPER BLISS

AB👄UT

THAT

KISS

OTHER HARPER BLISS NOVELS
At Your Most Beautiful
A Breathless Place
If You Kiss Me Like That
Two Hearts Trilogy
Next in Line for Love
A Lesson in Love
Life in Bits (with T.B. Markinson)
A Swing at Love (with Caroline Bliss)
Once Upon a Princess (with Clare Lydon)
In the Distance There Is Light
The Road to You
Far from the World We Know
Seasons of Love
Release the Stars
At the Water's Edge
High Rise (The Complete Collection)

THE PINK BEAN SERIES
THE FRENCH KISSING SERIES

CHAPTER ONE
FAYE

"Tell me again why I'm doing this, darling?" I ask Brandon.

He flicks his long hair behind his shoulder and looks me straight in the eye. "You're doing it for me, Faye."

Why this man isn't an A-list actor yet, I have no idea. He delivers the line with the authenticity of the best in the business.

"That's right. It's all for you." I paint on a smile, which flees my face as the car comes to an abrupt halt.

Brandon waves it off with a flick of his wrist. "Los Angeles traffic."

My phone buzzes in my pocket. It must be Leslie. She promised she'd call me on the way to the table read. I wonder which of her two top clients she called first—me or Ida Burton?

"Hi, Faye, you're going to kill it in the read-through. I know it."

"Thanks, Leslie."

"I just got off the phone with Ida." That answers my question then. "She's looking forward to it a lot."

"Is she?" Even if she wasn't, she wouldn't have told the agent we share. She's probably as nervous as I am. Three Best Actor Oscars on my mantel don't make any difference to my trepidation on the way to the very first table read, especially for a movie like this one. It doesn't help that my co-star, Ida Burton, has four golden statuettes to her name.

"Of course, she is. Everyone's excited about this. The whole of Hollywood is buzzing."

"Christ, Leslie. What did you have for breakfast this morning?"

"My usual three espressos," she says with a level tone.

"Okay." I could barely stomach the nut-and-berry mix Brandon prepares for me every morning. "Good to know."

"Call me if you need anything," Leslie says. "I'm always here for you."

Because there isn't that much else to say, we end the conversation. I glance at Brandon for comfort. He isn't just my personal assistant, but also one of the most entertaining people I know, which says a lot when you work in Hollywood. He's very good at giving pep talks when I need them, but he also, instinctively, knows when it's best to shut up.

He leans toward me and puts his hand on my knee. "Playing gay is all the rage these days. And the script is hilarious. For once, it's not one of those bleak movies where the lesbians stomp through their lives looking like they're never getting any." He sends me a smile. "Hollywood has finally realized that lesbians can have a sense of humor too." He follows up with a chuckle.

"It's not playing a lesbian that's got me so wound up. It's

2

playing one opposite Ida Burton." In the first half of the movie, my character, Mindy, is straight as an arrow.

"Ida Burton hasn't been in a hit movie in over a decade. If anything, she should be worried about starring in a movie with you." He shrugs. "She's practically B-list now." He brings a hand in front of his mouth, as though suddenly realizing his utter sacrilege.

"We both know Ida Burton will never come close to being B-list, no matter how little her movies gross."

"You never know," Brandon says. "This town can be cruel."

The car comes to a complete stop. We've arrived at the hotel where the *A New Day* table read is taking place. The driver opens the door for us. I take a deep breath and get out. A member of the production staff is waiting for me. I follow her inside, Brandon hot on my heels.

The first person I recognize is Charlie, who's basically to blame for all of this. Not only did she co-write the script, but me being her wife's maid of honor at their wedding last year would have made me look like a stone-cold hypocrite if I'd refused to take this part because it's a lesbian movie.

Charlie's basically jumping out of her skin with excitement. She hugs me tightly and the nervous tension shimmers in her muscles.

"You look like a million bucks, Faye," she says.

Before I can thank her, the energy in the room changes. That can only mean one thing. The great Ida Burton has arrived. I turn around and am met with her famously blinding smile. Even I, not exactly a B-lister myself, am momentarily dazed by it. What is it with this woman and her smile?

Admittedly, in one of my lesser moments, I once tried to

emulate it in front of the mirror, but a smile of such radiance and assurance is not something that can be taught, nor practiced. Ida Burton was born with it and she's made a damn good career out of it. Add to that a luxurious mass of copper-colored curly hair, brown Bambi eyes, and a voice to melt the sturdiest of glaciers, and you have the marvelous Ida Burton. It's hard not to feel as though I'm standing in her shadow.

After saying a few quick hellos, she walks straight toward me.

"Faye. *Hiiii!*" Ida sounds as though seeing me is the highlight of her year.

"Ida." We exchange two featherlight cheek kisses. "I've been looking forward to this." It's not a lie. I have. Maybe not the feeling of having to play second fiddle to Ida, but working on this hot-as-hell movie.

"So have I." She flashes me that smile again. How can her skin look so impossibly smooth? We're about the same age, but Ida makes me feel like I'm at least ten years her senior.

"Ladies." Tamara, the director, has joined us. "It's so good to see you again. I'm raring to go. You have no idea." She points at two chairs next to each other. "Those are your seats. We'll start in fifteen minutes. Refreshments are over there." She nods in the direction of the buffet. "I'm here if you have any questions." She takes a step back. "I'll let you acclimatize first."

Behind me, Brandon is whispering with Ida's assistant, Mark, whom he has told me all about because they had a thing once. Brandon likes to keep me apprised of his love life. Maybe he thinks it somehow makes up for the lack of romance I have in my own life.

For the past twenty years, I've always been the biggest

star in the room at a table read, and it has fallen upon me to put my co-stars at ease. Today, I'm not sure this task is up to me.

"I'm a little nervous." Ida surprises me. "I think this could be a great movie, but... well, I've seen things go horribly wrong before, no matter how promising the screenplay."

She's wearing a beige top that accentuates the fiery color of her hair. Even though she's dressed quite casually in slacks and said top, a glow seems to emanate from her. An effortless star quality.

"This seems like the kind of project the studio would want to keep a tight grip on."

"We can only do what's required of us," Ida says.

"Play gay," I lamely joke.

Ida shuffles her weight around. "Correct." She pins her gaze on me. "I was really thrilled to hear you were on board. Even though it really shouldn't be, it's still a risk to play a part like this. Especially for someone like you."

"Not just me." I emit a nervous chuckle. "For you as well, no doubt."

"For both of us then," she confirms and quirks up the corner of her mouth. "We should have dinner. Discuss our characters and their emotional arcs."

"Uh, yeah. Sure. We should."

"I'll have my guy call your guy." She eyes our PAs. "I assume you know they have history?"

I nod. "In the greatest detail." My smile, though wide and generous, feels lacking compared to hers.

"Oh, god. Does he tell you everything as well? Mark does too. The latest is that he's ready to settle down. Maybe he and his new man will start a family and he won't have time to be my assistant anymore."

The things we worry about, I think, although I recognize her attachment to her assistant. I've worked with Brandon for almost ten years, which is a lifetime in assistant years. I wouldn't know what to do with myself if he left, even though I would be the first to urge him to try for greater things than being at my beck and call.

"His life—" I say.

"I really—" she starts at the same time.

"You go first." Despite all the glamour that surrounds her, Ida is refreshingly down-to-earth.

"I really enjoyed your performance in *Night Break*," she says. "I see another Oscar in your future."

I wave her off because that's what you're meant to do, even though ever since that movie premiered, all I've heard is chatter about winning an Oscar for it. If I could get an actual man called Oscar for it, that would be a million times better than another statue in my living room. A statue doesn't give me affection, nor does it reply when I address it.

"What was it like working with Silke Meisner?"

"Amazing." That's Hollywood-speak for grueling but just rewarding enough in the end. I'm sure Ida has been through the same and if there's one person in this room who will catch my drift, it's her.

She nods thoughtfully. "Tell me all about it when you come to dinner."

"Sure."

She cocks her head. "Things are going to get quite intimate between us on set." Her voice does a funny thing.

"Just a bit of mild kissing." I try to sound casual. Apart from a girl I pecked on the lips decades ago, I have zero experience kissing women, although I can't imagine it being much different from kissing a male co-star. But the first woman I'm ever going to kiss properly, albeit for the sake of make-believe, is Ida Burton.

She erupts into a chuckle. "Good to know you're cool with that."

"I wouldn't be doing this movie if I weren't." And I would be a flaming homophobe, my friend Ava told me in no uncertain terms.

"Ladies," the director approaches us again. "Ready when you are."

CHAPTER TWO

IDA

Does anyone notice how I'm dying on the inside? How I'm regretting taking this part? How my dubious ulterior motive is already catching up with me big time?

Faye Fleming sits beside me in all her girl-next-door glory, although she's hardly a girl anymore. Still, as she has aged, she's managed to maintain the image of the all-American, wholesome, funny-but-serious-when-needed girl/woman. I guess of all the people gathered here, she and I might become the closest. How long will it take her to figure out my secret?

"Ida," Tamara says, "would you like to give us your thoughts on your character? Or do you want to launch straight into the read?"

Ah, my character. An out-and-proud lesbian. If only I could express my true feelings about Veronica to the room.

"Sure." I've prepared for this. I know exactly what to say so as not to cast any suspicion on myself. "I see Veronica as a successful but, ultimately, lonely woman who is starved of love." At times, while I was reading the script, I wondered if the writers had been able to glimpse right into the center of my own lonesome heart. "Her brother's fourth wedding sparks this unbridled rage in her, as though all the love in her family, and the world even, is reserved for him, just because he's straight." I pause. "She's so consumed by anger and jealousy that she doesn't even notice that her own chance at love is staring her right in the face. She needs to get over that, and some other things, of course. Crack a few jokes along the way." I insert a chuckle. My inadequate synopsis does not do justice to the script, which is, apart from being a lesbian romantic comedy, also a sharply funny critique on the institution of marriage.

"Charlie? Liz?" Tamara says. "Does that sound about right to you?"

"Perfect," a blond woman with huge round eyes says. The one sitting next to her, who was all over the news five years ago when she started an affair with Ava Castaneda, nods and sends me a nervous smile. I should be the one smiling timidly at her. For all my money, she has something I've never been able to afford.

"Great," Tamara says. "We'll come back to this later, if needed. Faye, shall we move on to your character?"

"My character doesn't have a clue," Faye says, eliciting her first and surely not her last round of easy laughs. Why Faye is playing the more uptight character in this movie, I have no idea. That's why it's called acting, I suppose.

The read-through of the first act is easy enough. Faye and I play off each other with a comfort I've rarely experienced this quickly, as if we've starred together countless times before.

During the break before we run through the second act, Tamara walks up to me.

"The chemistry between you and Faye is off the charts already," she says, "and we haven't even gotten to the good bits yet."

There's a moment in the second act that I've been dreading. My character, Veronica, needs to look Faye's character in the eye and realize something significant that alters the course of events. It's not something I would usually have an issue with conveying, nor is it required that I display all of that complex emotion at a table read, but still. It all hits a little too close to home. Today, I'll be able to muddle through, but I don't know how I'm going to approach it at rehearsals. But that's exactly what rehearsals are for, I comfort myself. To figure out that kind of stuff.

"Thanks." I take the opportunity to get a good look at Tamara. No doubt she's one of the hottest directors I've worked with, what with ninety percent of the ones I've previously collaborated with having been male. But it's not because the bar is low that Tamara isn't, objectively speaking, highly attractive. On top of that, just like my character, she's out and proud like nobody's business. These days, that can get you a top job behind the camera in Hollywood. How things have changed.

Someone calls for her and as she walks away, I make a mental note to ask Mark whether Tamara's love life is happier than my character's—or mine.

When I sit next to Faye again, with her long dark hair and pale complexion, her eyes as blue as the midday sky outside, I try to center myself and remember the reasons why I said yes to this project.

There are many and I list them in my head. This movie is being touted as next summer's big blockbuster and I haven't been part of one of those in a long time. My name next to Faye Fleming's should add up to more than the sum of its parts. Maybe, by playing an out character, I can finally force myself out of the closet. Maybe I won't even have to. Maybe the buzz surrounding the movie will create some sort of magic momentum that will naturally propel me out and make it so that it has always just been plain obvious.

Fat chance of that.

I make quick work of having to look Faye in the eye—just a swift glance will have to do. Today isn't about looks and gestures and emotions. It's about making sure the words sound right as they come out of our mouths.

I already know Faye is an accomplished actor, but even more than that, she's a calming presence by my side. She comes across as self-confident and easy-going and I have no way of knowing whether she's acting or not, but in the end, it doesn't matter. The overall vibe is that she will be easy to work with. No diva allures whatsoever. It must be the girl-next-door thing. Maybe she's made it part of her real-life persona as well as her image. Imagine if Faye Fleming had to bust out of the closet. The thought appears to be too much for my brain.

"Sparks are flying," Tamara says after we've finished. "Can't wait for the actual shoot."

"How was it?" Derek, my best friend and ex-husband asks when I call him on the way home.

"Good." I sink into the leather car seat. "Although I forgot how utterly exhausting table reads are."

"You go through the emotions of the entire movie in one day," he says. "It's to be expected."

I asked Derek to read the script before I said yes to the movie.

"How was Faye Fleming?" he asks.

"Lovely, also as to be expected." So far, I can't say a bad word about my co-star. She was gracious and wonderful to be around all day long, even during the final exhausting hours. "I'll have her over for dinner soon, so we can get to know each other better before we start rehearsals."

"Before you kiss her, you mean," my ex-husband says.

Derek is one of the only people on this planet who knows my secret. As I was once the only person who knew his.

"Very funny."

"I'm just teasing, although you could have worse prospects." He's not one to let things go easily.

"The director's quite hot, actually." Derek's the only person I can talk to about these things.

"Tell me more." Although Derek and I were never in love, we have a deep fondness for one another and I know that what he wants for me more than anything else is to find true love the way he has with his boyfriend, Ben.

"I haven't done my research yet and, well, you know…"

"I know this movie has the potential to change your life. What's this director's name again? I'll do a quick search for you."

13

"Tamara Williams, but no need. I'm perfectly capable of googling the details of her personal life myself."

"But it's more fun when I do it." There's a short pause, before Derek speaks again. "It says here she's married. Sorry, sweetie."

"Oh well, perhaps it's for the best."

"I see that differently, but we all need the time we need…"

We say our goodbyes and as my car glides up Mulholland, I vividly remember the statement I put out after Derek came out of the closet.

I wish Derek all the luck and love in the world. We had a wonderful marriage and we remain the best of friends. I know this new path he has chosen in life will make him very happy.

I got a lot of flak at the time for using the phrase 'the new path he has chosen in life', as though I meant to say that him being gay was a choice. If only it were—then I wouldn't have had to hide in the corner of a stifling closet for the better part of my life.

What I meant was that he had chosen to end our marriage and no longer pretend he was straight. And no longer care about the repercussions on his career. The hoops I had to jump through to explain that. Yes, my choice of words was poor, and no, I did not mean all the things that the wave of social media outrage claimed I did.

Perhaps I should have taken the opportunity to come out there and then, but I didn't. Because, unlike Derek, I do care about the effect it would have on my career—at least I used to. Seeing Derek blossom into the proud and confident man he is today with Ben by his side has made me aware of the possible error of my ways. How could it not while I'm the one who remains single in my golden cage of a Hollywood Hills mansion?

When this car drops me off, no one will be waiting for me. Mark has gone home for the day. In my absence, my house will have been scrubbed clean and my lawn will have been cut and my pool will have been cleaned, and for what?

That's why I've chosen to do this movie. That's why I've chosen to play an out character, hoping that it will become one of those cases of life imitating art.

This is Hollywood and far stranger things have happened.

CHAPTER THREE
FAYE

Tradition has it that, if she's in town, my best friend Ava prepares me a post-table-read feast for dinner. Not only is she in town, but her wife is one of the writers of the movie, so I'm expecting Ava to have gone all out tonight. We're neighbors and to get to Ava's house all I have to do is walk along the beach for a minute.

"Is it just you?" I ask, when I kiss her hello on the deck overlooking the ocean.

"Charlie's with Liz. She said not to expect her home before midnight. Apparently, the table-read has brought some screenplay issues to light that can only be fixed tonight."

I bring a hand to my chest in mock horror. "I hope my performance wasn't too inadequate."

Ava pours me a glass of Cristal and hands it to me. "You know it's not you."

"Just one drink tonight. Starring alongside Ida Burton..." I shake my head. "I don't know."

"Tell me about her." We sit, and I stare at the lowering

sun reflecting on the surface of the ocean for a few moments. No matter how stressful a day, coming home to Malibu and being near the water always calms me. Sitting next to Ava with a glass of champagne in my hand also helps.

"She was perfectly lovely, but…" I sigh because I know I will sound like the biggest Hollywood cliché. "She looked so damn good. Like she'd been through full hair and makeup. It was only a table read, goddammit."

Ava chuckles. "Did she make you feel outshined?"

I nod. I wouldn't admit this to many other people and I'm secretly glad Charlie's not here, although Ava will probably tell her later. One of the things I've always liked most about Ava Castaneda is that she has never taken any of this Hollywood bullshit seriously. She has always done exactly as she pleased without caring about the possible consequences to her image and her employment. It hasn't made any difference because, even though her house might be more modest than mine, it's still a Malibu beach house and the view is exactly the same.

"I wrongly assumed I was at the top of the pecking order, what with Ida not having had a hit in so long, but… when she walks into a room, everything stops. The vibe changes completely. It's like she has this magnetic forcefield around her. I watched some of her older movies to prepare and even in the worst, most cringeworthy ones, she dazzles. She lifts up the entire movie. It's crazy."

"Yet, she's not the blockbuster machine you are."

"She just hasn't worked as much as I have."

"Hence, you should be rewarded for all your hard work and get top billing for this one." Ava leans toward me. "I'll tell Charlie to treat you with more deference," she jokes.

"Please, don't. It's all good, you know. I'm not interested in a Hollywood cat fight about who gets more attention on set. But you know this movie has me more nervous than others."

"I know, Faye, but it really shouldn't. Look at what *Underground* has done for Elisa Fox. Playing gay is not the death sentence it used to be to an actor's career—on the contrary. Elisa's the best paid actor in the world because of her part in *Underground*."

"Still. It's different."

"We've been over this a million times." Ava was the one who convinced me it was time for someone 'of my caliber' to do this movie. The fact that her wife co-wrote it might have also had something to do with it.

"I know. I need to get used to the idea, now that it's all becoming very real. Having just read the entire manuscript out loud makes it real. Now I'm in this weird, kind of stressful limbo before shooting starts."

"Look at it from a different perspective. You're privileged to be able to play this part. Even Ida Burton wants to come out of semi-retirement to be in it. You have no idea how lucky you are." She drums her fingertips on the table, then says, "I asked Charlie if I could audition for the part of Veronica." Ava huffs out some air through her teeth.

"You did?"

The finger drumming becomes more agitated.

"What happened?" This is the first I've heard of this. Ava's been up and down about wanting to pursue a career in acting for as long as I've known her.

"What happened is that I almost filed for divorce."

I straighten my spine and look at her in disbelief. "Why?"

"You know Charlie. She can be insufferable sometimes."

Charlie is one of the sweetest people I've come across in this town. "What did she say?"

"Charlie believes she has this sixth sense when it comes to actors and their acting abilities and according to her, I don't have the required ability."

"Oh my god." Charlie's brave, I give her that, but perhaps also a little insensitive to what her wife wants to hear. "She actually said that to you?"

Ava nods. "This was before Ida was even in the picture for the part of Veronica." She shrugs, but I can tell it still stings.

"Did you really want to audition for the part?" Now that I've done the table-read opposite Ida, it has become impossible to imagine anyone else as Veronica—such is the power of Ida Burton. "Why didn't you tell me?"

"Because…" She expels another deep sigh. "After I told my wife—the woman I married and who is supposed to love me and believe in me more than anyone else—and my beloved wife proceeded to tell me to stop dreaming already, how could I possibly make even more of a fool of myself by telling anyone else, let alone Faye Fleming?"

"Are you okay about this?"

"I shouldn't have tried to muscle in on Charlie's movie, I do get that." Her tone conveys some unprocessed hurt. "She and Liz wrote it with the purpose of casting massive A-listers like yourself and Ida. But still. A little more spousal support would have been nice."

"Charlie adores you, though."

"As she should." Some glee is starting to come through Ava's voice again.

"So you're not getting a divorce any time soon?" I still feel like I should make certain.

Ava scoffs. "I'm not going to divorce her now, am I? This movie's bound to be an even bigger hit than *Underground*."

"If Ida and I don't mess it up." I relax my shoulders. Ava's probably been laying it on thick, but I'm no expert at relationships so it's good to have reassurance. "I can put you in touch with the best acting coaches in the business, if you want."

"I *should* get really good at acting behind her back, if only to prove Charlie wrong." Ava empties her glass. "But what if she's right, though?"

"Didn't you just renew your *Knives Out* contract for another three seasons?" I hold up my almost empty champagne flute.

"That I did." Ava tops up our drinks, ignoring what I said earlier about only having the one. "Now let's talk about something other than work." She pins her gaze on me. "Any eligible men in the room for you today? Who plays Veronica's brother again?"

"Robert Glazer," I say.

Ava mulls this over. "He's cute. Is he single?"

"I have no idea," I say half-chuckling. "But I'm really not interested in starting some on-set romance. I'm not interested in starting any kind of romance..." I pause. I want to tell Ava something else. Something I haven't told anyone. "I've been thinking about making a change in my life."

"What's that?"

I glance at her sideways. She stares straight ahead. I follow her example. Everything is more easily divulged when staring at the ocean.

"Adoption."

Her face turns swiftly in my direction. Her eyes are wide as she glances at me. "For real?"

"Human adoption," I specify. "As in a child. Not a cat or dog."

"Damn." She narrows her eyes. "I did not see that coming, Faye, but yeah, why not?"

"Because becoming a single mother is terrifying," I say. "Because there are so many unknown factors. Because I have no idea if I'd be any good at parenting."

"Have you taken any concrete steps?"

I shake my head. "I know I haven't got that much time to waste, what with me swiftly approaching fifty."

"You don't have to adopt a newborn baby, unless that's what you want," Ava says.

"It's tough figuring out all of this on my own."

"You don't have to do it on your own. You know I'm always here for you." Ava turns to me fully. "I'm glad you told me."

"I'll do this movie first and then I'll make my final decision. Then, I either do it or I don't." I look away briefly. "After Brian and I tried to conceive and it never happened—even after we separated—the thought of becoming a mother has always stayed with me, like this tiny fire burning deep inside me. It's been flickering for more than ten years now. It makes me wonder what I've been afraid of for so long."

"It's a big decision and, well, things happen. Time passes. Before you know it, you're fifty years old."

"I do know that I want it. It's not the desire to be a mother that I doubt. It's whether I'll be a good one that's holding me back."

"If every potential parent thought like that, none of us would be here."

"Yeah, but you know what I mean. I have money and I

have privilege and, god knows, so much love to give, but there are no guarantees."

"Darling." Ava puts a hand on my arm. "Look at me."

I turn my gaze away from the ocean and look into Ava's beautifully peaceful face.

"There's no doubt in my mind you will be the world's best mother. I mean it. You're kind and smart and funny. You're Faye fucking Fleming. Any child you adopt will be the luckiest little prince or princess on this planet."

I erupt into a chuckle. "If you put it like that."

"How else am I going to convey the truth?" Ava says this so matter-of-factly, I have no choice but to believe her.

CHAPTER FOUR

IDA

"Why did you decide to take the leap, so to speak, and do this movie?" I ask Faye Fleming, whilst expertly hiding my own motive.

"My friend Ava told me to do it already," she says, as though it makes perfect sense. Of course, I know who Ava Castaneda is and I also know that her wife co-wrote *A New Day*. The internet nearly broke when Ava Castaneda came out five years ago. "She said it was time, you know?" Faye pops an olive into her mouth and licks her finger. The lamp behind her makes her hair look like a soft-glowing halo.

"I'm not sure I do know."

"It's time for actors like you and me to play in a movie like that," Faye says.

"I guess Ava was right."

"You must think so as well, otherwise why would you have decided to do it?" Faye is very direct. I wonder if this will cause problems between us down the line.

I can't tell her I have my own reasons, although I do realize that for my life to actually change because of this movie, I will have to start telling other people things I've kept secret about myself forever. But my co-star in the movie is not the person to tell. We might share an agent and have traveled in the same circles for a long time, but I barely know Faye. She's here to change that.

"Oh, yes, of course I believe that very much as well. Representation in movies and on TV is so important," I regurgitate Derek's line. "Look at *Underground*. Nothing but lesbians in that." My love for *Underground* knows no bounds. I was secretly hoping its lead, Elisa Fox who plays chief spy Aretha in the show, would co-star in this movie with me, but you can hardly call playing next to Faye Fleming settling for less.

"I love *Underground* as much as the next person, but it hasn't exactly set off an avalanche of people coming out in Tinseltown."

A knot coils in my stomach. "Maybe not, but it has changed something. It has created a more open-minded atmosphere, at least."

"Can I ask you something... private?" She paints on a conspiratorial smile.

My heart hammers against my chest. "Sure." Surely, she won't ask me *that*.

"Because of your ex, you must know... more than most." She leans over the table as though it isn't just the two of us in my house. "I know of two male and one female closeted A-list actors."

My heart's about to explode right out of my chest. She can't possibly be referring to me.

"They lead these terribly complicated double lives." She shakes her head. "I mean, the energy it must take to hold up that façade all the time and to never be yourself as soon as you leave the safety of your house." She reaches for another olive. Her posture is casual. Her tone is soft rather than interrogating. She's just confiding in me, not confronting me. "It's astounding."

I try to take a deep, calming breath without Faye noticing. "It is. It's, uh, a bit nuts. Yeah." *Oh, Christ, Ida. Get a grip.*

"Do you know of anyone?" Her gaze finds mine for an instant. "You and Derek are still friendly, aren't you?"

"We are, yes. Very much." If Derek were a fly on the wall for this conversation, he would be in stitches right now. This is exactly why I came out of that damned closet, he would say. That and the obvious fact that closets are vertical coffins. I can so easily hear my ex-husband's voice in my head. "And yes, I think I might know who you're talking about."

Faye's eyes narrow. "Are we naming names?"

"Erm, no. I don't think we should," I'm quick to say.

"Why? If we both know?"

Because I'd like anyone else to extend me the same courtesy, I think. "Put yourself in their shoes. Would you like to be talked about in that way?"

"In what way?" Faye shrugs. "They're gay. That's it."

"I know what you mean, but take this movie for example. I'm sure Leslie sat you down and gave you the same speech she gave me. And that means that being gay in Hollywood isn't simply being-gay-and-that's-it. As much as it pains me to say that and as absurd as it is in this day and age, especially in the entertainment industry, which is basically run by gays."

"Fair point, but that's why we're doing this movie. To contribute, as straight allies, what we can to change this ridiculous status quo."

I swallow hard. I know very well that coming out would be the most powerful contribution I could make, instead of cowardly posing as a straight ally, but as Derek said on the phone the other day: we all need the time we need.

Faye seems to have forgotten about naming names, which is good, because although I can try to read her all I like, I still have no way of knowing whether the female actor she was referring to was me. It's probably Lily Matthews though, whose sexual orientation is one of Hollywood's worst kept secrets, which is one of the reasons I've always stayed far away from her.

"But as long as we're on the subject," Faye says. "Can I ask about you and Derek?"

My heart leaps all the way into my throat again. "There's really not that much to say," I try. Most people know not to push it further when faced with this line from me. Faye doesn't seem like the type. She's not impressed by my stardom. In fact, she sees right through it.

"Did you know when you married him that he was gay?"

If I weren't so terrified of it, I would admire her directness. "No, of course not," I lie.

"Did *he* know he was gay?"

"Derek's still one of my best friends. I don't feel comfortable discussing his private life."

"I'm more interested in *your* private life, anyway," Faye says. "I don't know what's worse. Being married to a gay man and not knowing it, like you, or flitting from one failed relationship to the next with absolutely nothing to show for it but heartache after heartache, like me."

My hackles are all the way up but a lifetime of not talking about myself has made me an excellent listener—a quality not often found in my profession. I sense that there's an opening to shift the subject away from my love life to Faye's, which, if the tabloid press is to be believed, is nothing to write home about.

"I take it you're single?" I try to keep my tone light but inviting.

"Have been for a good long while now," she says on a sigh. "Honestly, if I'd known in advance how difficult it is to find a good man when you're... in our position. I'm not sure I would have signed up for it. I know it sounds ridiculously conceited, but fame does come at a price. A big one."

I nod because it's true. I pay the price every day. "I'm sorry that part of your life hasn't worked out the way you wanted it to."

"At least you've been married, which is more than I can say." She shoots me a devilish grin. "Although he turned out to be gay." She cocks her head. "You did... consummate the marriage?" She shakes her head and holds up her hand. "Sorry, none of my business."

As much as I care for Derek, the idea of sleeping with him has always made me laugh more than anything else. Neither one of us ever entertained the notion. Out of habit, I nod, even though it's a flagrant lie. But that was the deal Derek and I made when we got married. Why would we even have bothered with the whole charade if we weren't going to milk it for all it was worth?

"Ah, men, can't live with them and can't live without them," Faye says.

"I guess that's what your character in *A New Day* would say."

"Except that the script is written by two of Hollywood's top writers and they don't use cliché lines like that." Faye leans back in her chair.

"It's the jokes that gave me the final push to do the movie. So many comedies these days are only trying to be funny and not succeeding whatsoever. This one's genuinely funny and it has something to say."

"And we get to kiss," Faye says, giggling like a schoolgirl.

"There's that." From experience, I know how awkward and down-right annoying it is to kiss a co-star in front of the camera. But I've never had to kiss a woman on set before.

"Are you nervous about that?" Her question seems genuine enough.

"A bit," I answer truthfully.

"Have you, um, ever kissed a woman before?" Her eyes twinkle.

Oh, Jesus. The obvious answer is no, although of course I have kissed a woman before and all I ever want to do for the rest of my life is kiss other women. But in this life—the one I've constructed for myself—it's impossible to do without wielding a non-disclosure agreement in the other woman's face. And that's not something that advances the course of romance.

"Ida?" Faye pulls me from my reverie. "I'm sorry if that was too forward. I didn't mean to make you feel uncomfortable. If anything, I was trying to break the ice before rehearsals."

"No, no, please, I'm the one who's sorry." I suck my bottom lip between my teeth and bite down a little. Just to remind myself that this is my one and only real life and it doesn't have to be glued together with lies any longer. "I have…" I can't look Faye in the eye when I make this admission. "I have kissed a woman before."

"On set or…"

"For real." I follow up with a slow nod. Part of me wants to reveal more, but something coils in my gut and my throat swells with dryness. I take a quick sip of water. "It didn't mean anything. It was one of those things you do when you're young and foolish." My throat constricts as I speak the last words, as though it is so fed up with all my lies, it doesn't want to cooperate any longer.

"Same here."

Is Faye looking at me differently? I don't know. I'm probably seeing her differently now that I've come so close, but remain so very far away from who I really am. Decades of hiding make it hard for me to be in full view. It has never been where I've thrived, despite my chosen profession in the spotlight.

"I barely remember it, to be honest," Faye continues "It happened light- years ago. I'm ashamed to say I don't even remember the other woman's name."

If only I didn't remember the last woman I kissed. Her name was Martha. Even though the last time I kissed her—a long and dreadful kiss goodbye—was years ago, I remember it as though it happened yesterday. The softness of her lips. The sadness in her eyes—and in my heart. And for what? So I could sit here with Faye Fleming and lie to her face as well?

CHAPTER FIVE
FAYE

It's the third day of rehearsals when Tamara announces that she wants to focus on the kissing scene—not the actual kiss, but what comes before and after.

She takes Ida and me to one side to go over the scene with us.

"Mindy appears like she doesn't have a clue, even though she has picked up on certain things Veronica has said. She's not stupid," Tamara says. "For the record, Faye, I don't think you're stupid either." She inserts a chuckle. "I know you know this, but I just want to make sure we're on the same page."

So far, Tamara has been a dream to work with. She knows what she wants but she's not obnoxious about it. She does what the best directors I know do effortlessly. She makes it all come together while bringing out the best in her actors and crew. As far as rehearsals go, she's already done a great job in making it clear that she's in complete control of her craft and she knows exactly how she's going to get the actors to portray her vision for this movie.

The scene is pivotal because it's when the movie shifts into more romantic territory and it represents a huge gear change as well as an increase in on-screen chemistry between Ida and me.

"I've got it," I say. It's often harder to say exactly what my character will do than to actually do it. "You'll see." This is one of the reasons why we take the time to rehearse so thoroughly. It isn't all about blocking the shots and testing the lights—stand-ins are used for that, anyway. It's about hitting the right emotional tone and establishing a rapport between the characters.

"Can't wait," Tamara says, then turns to Ida. "Veronica has been going completely nuts for days now."

I study Ida as Tamara clarifies some key aspects of this scene for her. Ida has seemed a bit off since she arrived this morning. Her smile isn't as wide and her laugh not as bright as usual.

Ida nods yet she looks absentminded.

"Do you need some time?" Tamara asks.

"No, no. I'm fine," Ida insists. "Let's do this." Even her voice is a touch shaky. Or maybe she has found a way of making herself extra vulnerable for the scene. Maybe that's the kind of actor she is, although this is the first time I've noticed it. Maybe she's been saving it for this first more emotional scene that we're rehearsing. So yes, I conclude, it must be that. Ida's simply being a pro. What does that make me? Just someone with a different method of conveying emotions, I assure myself.

"Okay," Tamara says and escorts us to our places. "Action, please."

I recite my lines with a little help from the script. This isn't about saying the words exactly as they appear on the page just yet. For me, this is more about getting the feeling behind the words and the interaction with my co-star right.

"Be nice to your brother," I say, as Mindy. "This may be his fourth wife, but you're his only sister." I glance at Ida as Veronica. Her demeanor is more Ida than Veronica. Veronica is supposed to take a step closer to Mindy, but Ida doesn't move. She's not responding to my line at all.

"Ida?" Tamara asks. "Do you need a break? Or do we need to talk through this scene more?"

"Uhm. No. I mean, maybe." We've only been working in close proximity for a few days, yet I can tell something's upsetting Ida. She's trying to sound as though everything's fine, while it's obviously not. I have no clue what's going on with her, but it strikes me as odd for someone like Ida Burton to turn up for rehearsals so unprepared. There goes my earlier theory of her making herself vulnerable for this key scene. "I'm sorry," Ida says. "This is terribly unprofessional of me. Let's just try again."

"Hey, it's okay," I whisper. "This isn't my favorite scene either."

Her mouth scrunches into a tense pout. She takes a deep breath.

I find Tamara's gaze and she nods at me. I repeat my line and look at Ida, waiting. Again, nothing happens. It's like she's freezing. Like something inside is stopping her from interacting with me in this scene.

"Oh, crap." Ida drops her hands. "I'm so embarrassed about this. Mark!" She glances around for her assistant. "I'm going to need a minute."

"Everyone, take five," Tamara yells.

Ida rushes off with Mark. I have nothing better to do than find Brandon, who hands me a bottle of water.

"What's going on?" he asks.

"Beats me."

"It's pretty obvious to me." He stands there smirking.

"Oh, really?"

"She doesn't want to kiss you, Faye." He leans in closer and inspects my mouth. "Hm, is there something on your lips. Show me your teeth. Are they clean?"

I roll my eyes at his silliness, although I know he's only doing it to blow off some steam. "We're not actually kissing today, just rehearsing the scene."

"You're still getting pretty close."

"Do you think I should go talk to her?"

Brandon shakes his head, his long hair swaying behind him. "No, best leave her alone for a bit. Let her gather herself. She's Ida Burton, for crying out loud. I'm sure she'll return raring to go." He holds me in his gaze. "Ready to maul you."

Charlie walks up to us. "Is it the lines, do you think? They're not flowing as well as I thought they were."

"I don't think so," I say.

"When Ida comes back, let's just run through them quickly, more like another read-through, to get her into it. Okay?"

"Good idea."

"We'll take it from there. See how it goes." Charlie waggles her eyebrows. "It's easy enough to write, but I fully acknowledge it's so much harder to act."

"I bet you had yourself some fun with this script." I might as well have some fun with Charlie. "By the way, Ava told me she wanted to audition for the part of Veronica, but you told her not to bother."

Charlie's eyes grow wide. "Oh, god, Faye," she groans. "I

wrongly assumed Ava would appreciate my honesty." She huffs out some air. "Only for it to turn into the biggest fight we've had since we got hitched."

"She'll get over it."

"Imagine you were playing opposite Ava instead of Ida." She cocks her head.

"Ava might not have such trouble gearing up to kiss me," I joke.

"I'm sure it's not you, Faye. How can it be?"

Tamara walks toward us with Ida and Mark behind her.

"Let's try the kissing scene again tomorrow and focus on the wedding today," she says.

I try to find Ida's gaze—she's going to have to look at me at some point—but she keeps her eyes to the floor.

"Sorry," Ida mouths when she does finally cut her glance to me. If Charlie's right and it's not me, then it can only be her.

CHAPTER SIX
IDA

"Fuck, fuck, fuck," is all I can say as I pace through Derek's living room. "I fucked up royally today."

"You're Ida Burton. No one will hold it against you, darling." He's trying to calm me down, but I can't stand still long enough for him to comfort me.

"That's exactly why I screwed up so much. Because I'm Ida Burton." I try to steady myself by looking out the window. The sky is steel-blue, not a cloud to be seen. "I need to call Leslie. I need to get out of this movie."

"Ida, please, calm down."

"You don't understand, Derek. I made such a fool of myself. I froze like a nervous first-year drama student with the worst case of stage fright. I can't go back there."

"You're a pro who had an off day."

"I think we both know that's not true." I finally slump into the couch, my legs as defeated as my spirit because my plan has backfired at the first hurdle. "I think we both know why I froze."

"Because you had to kiss Faye Fleming." The ice cube in

39

his glass of scotch rattles. "Frankly, I don't see the issue here."

I shoot him a cutting glance. If even Derek's not going to give me some sympathy for this, I really have no choice but to respectfully bow out. I pull my phone from my pocket and press the shortcut for Leslie. Derek hurries over to me and holds out his hand.

"Don't call your agent, Ida. Come on. You're not a teenage starlet with notions. You can do this."

The phone's already ringing and Leslie usually doesn't let it ring very long when I call, unless she's on the phone with Faye Fleming—maybe she called to complain about my unprofessional behavior and to ask what the hell is going on with me.

Just as I consider handing my phone to Derek, Leslie answers.

"Ida, darling, tell me how rehearsals are going." The thing with Leslie is that she can play dumb better than the finest actors I know. It's part of her agent spiel.

"I need you to get me out of this movie. I can't do it."

"What? Nonsense, Ida. You're perfect for that part."

"I'm absolutely horrible at it. I made a mistake accepting the role. I don't care how much it costs. I want out."

"Where are you?" Leslie's tone has gone from playful to code red.

"Derek's."

"I'm coming over to talk to you. I'll be there in half an hour. Meanwhile, think this through. Shooting starts in two weeks. It's not really an option to break your contract now."

"This is Hollywood. There are always options. I've had director changes *during* shoots. I've had co-stars pull out days before production. These things happen all the time."

"Not if I can help it." Leslie sounds as though she means business. "Stay put." With that, she's gone.

"There's no way Leslie's going to make this easy on you," Derek says. "And she shouldn't." He sits next to me. "Come on, talk to me."

"That's why I came to you. Because I don't have to explain."

"We've spent hours discussing this. I know it's not easy when you've hidden who you really are for so long, but let me tell you, Ida, life on the other side of this is so much better and brighter and more fulfilling. That's why you're doing this."

"That doesn't mean I have to do it on camera."

"True, but that's the decision you made. And it's not the only reason why you're doing this movie. This has the potential to put you fully back on the map. Don't pull out now. You will regret it. I know it."

"Easy for you to say." I can hear the self-pity in my voice.

"That's a bit of a low blow. You know very well it's been far from easy for me, which is why you're doing things differently."

"I've just... never frozen like that. Like a deer in the headlights. It's like I felt everyone's eyes on me, even people who weren't there, like my mother and my brother. Like everyone was watching me closely to see the real meaning behind that kiss." I slap my palm on my thigh. "But the real kicker is that Tamara didn't even ask us to rehearse the actual kiss. Just the lines leading up to it."

"You're scared." Derek puts his arm around my shoulder. "It's perfectly normal because all of this is scary."

"Not so much in the grand scheme of things."

Derek shakes his head adamantly. "Coming out in Hollywood is no small thing. It should be, but it isn't."

My phone starts ringing. I expect it to be Leslie telling me she's stuck in traffic, but Faye Fleming's name appears on my screen. I show Derek my lit-up phone.

"Pick up, damn it," he urges me.

Reluctantly, I do. "Hi, Faye. Sorry again for today," I launch into an apology straightaway. "I truly don't know what came over me," I lie. "Please know it had nothing to do with you whatsoever."

"Oh, of course I know that and don't worry about it. This stuff happens to the best of us and according to the number of Oscars you've won, you are the best of us."

"Fat load of good those did me today when it mattered."

"But that's just it. Today didn't matter all that much. We're not shooting yet."

"I know, but still." I do feel like I have some more groveling to do.

"Anyway, I have a proposition for you," Faye says. Is that the ocean I hear in the background?

"Oh?" My hands go a bit clammy.

"How about you come over to my house tonight and we go over the most difficult scenes. Just the two of us. No one watching. If only to just run through the lines again. Discuss what's going through our characters' heads."

I glance at Derek as though he can offer me advice. He sits there nodding like a maniac. Has he been listening to my call?

"Yes," he whispers. "Say yes, Ida."

"Okay." I pause. "Can I ask you something, though?"

"Shoot."

"Did Leslie put you up to this?" It would be a typical agent trick.

"Leslie? No. Why would she?" Faye has no reason to lie to me.

"No reason."

"I'll be expecting you, then." Faye's voice is as bright as her personality each time I've seen her. It must be easy existing in Hollywood without any big secrets. "I'm home, so any time's good."

"Thank you, Faye." I end the call. "Looks like I'm going over to Faye's for some kissing practice."

"I hate to say it, darling, but I think you need it," Derek says.

We burst into a giggle. Then I remember that my agent is on her way to talk some sense into me—while all it took was a phone call from Faye. I call her to tell her the crisis has been averted. For now. Because who knows how I will react when I turn up at Faye's?

Faye's Malibu house is on the beach and the roar of the waves is audible from her deck overlooking the Pacific. It's calming and exciting at the same time, although that might be how I feel inside. Seeing Faye does have a calming effect on me, but I'm also terribly nervous about how tonight will play out.

"Have you eaten?" she asks. "I have plenty of food in the house."

"I'm fine." I couldn't get a bite of anything past my throat right now if I tried.

"Glass of vino, perhaps?" She has dressed down in a

flimsy sundress through which I can see the contours of her underwear.

"I really shouldn't." I point at my face. "This skin isn't a magical wonder of nature."

"Maybe a small one to take the edge off." Maybe Faye needs to take the edge off as well.

I shake my head. "I feel like I need to do this in the same circumstances as the actual shoot and I have no intention of showing up to the set with a wine buzz."

"Got it." She gestures at the chairs and table. "Please, sit. I'll get us some water."

She must have sent home everyone who works for her. She wasn't kidding when she said no one would be watching. I breathe a sigh of relief because in this town you never know. There's always an assistant or agent or entourage member lurking around somewhere.

"Is it just us?" I want to make sure.

"Just us, as promised."

"Thank you so much for inviting me." I sound so solemn and serious—the opposite of the vibe of the movie we're trying to make.

"Consider it my co-star duty." She clinks her bottle of mineral water against mine.

"I've been around long enough to know that not all actors in this town think like that." It hits me how incredibly lovely Faye is.

"I think I've been around about as long as you have." Faye smiles at me. "We must have gone through a very similar journey."

Not a chance in hell, I think, unless Faye Fleming's been camping out in a plush but suffocating closet since she arrived in LA. I nod regardless.

We exchange some more chitchat but nerves prevent me from entering into a deeper level of conversation with her. I will only be able to relax after we've rehearsed.

"Shall we do this?" Faye asks, her voice soft and soothing.

"Let's." I unearth the wretched manuscript pages I've been struggling with. In the car on the way over, I managed to recite my lines without hesitation, but after what happened earlier today, I feel like I can't trust myself, which is not a good sensation to have running through you.

"Shall we just read it sitting down first?" Faye might have some director's blood in her. Many an actor fed up with having the camera trained on her has gone that route, but I think Faye enjoys the attention too much. You have to if you've stuck around for as long as we have, no matter the personal price you pay.

We run through the lines of the scene I froze in today without issue. Then we stand, put our scripts aside—because we know the text by heart by now after all the reciting we've done—and launch into the scene again. For real, this time.

"Be nice to your brother," Faye/Mindy says. "This may be his fourth wife, but you're his only sister."

I take a step closer to Faye and look her in the eye. "Don't you see, Mindy," I say, fully in character. "That's not what this is about."

She returns my gaze. "What is it about then?"

I look away. "It's about him—" Veronica gazes into Mindy's eyes again. "It's not about him." I swallow hard. "It's about you."

"What about me?" Faye/Mindy returns my gaze. Her eyes sparkle. I can tell she's fully in character.

"It's about this." I lean in closer. "It's about what I feel for you," I whisper. My face is so close to Faye's I can feel her breath. If Tamara were here, she'd end rehearsal now. But she's not here. It's just Faye and me and no one else. So I do what it says in the script. Without touching her anywhere else, I press my lips ever so lightly against hers. Faye must still be in character because she plays along. She follows the script and lets the kiss linger before pulling away.

Then, she does go off script.

CHAPTER SEVEN

FAYE

I touch a finger to my lips. Ida just kissed me. Or no, it wasn't Ida. It was Veronica. Even though that's how it's written in the script, I hadn't expected this and I'm the one who can't remember the next line.

"I'm sorry." I take a step back. If we can bring this kind of intensity to the shoot, Tamara will be beside herself. "My bad. I didn't realize we were going all the way," I say through a bout of horrifying giggles.

"Gosh, Faye. I—I was definitely in the moment. *Yay!*" Ida seems to be taken aback by it as well, even though she's the one who kissed me—or at least her character did. "Maybe I was too much in character just now?"

"No, look, it's fine. This is exactly what we were trying to accomplish. It's just that, after today, I didn't think we would get there so quickly."

"Let's maybe not include the kiss at rehearsals tomorrow," Ida says.

"Why did you include it now?" There's a sudden tension

in the air. I feel the acute need to deflate it with some banter. "Couldn't resist me?"

"You mean Mindy," Ida says.

"Sure." Just like I witnessed a subtle change in Ida's behavior at rehearsals today, I notice another shift right now. I can't put my finger on what it is exactly, but she's different than before. "We should probably do that again, minus the kiss and plus the lines I forgot."

"Hey, um, I'm sorry if that was out of line," Ida says. "I didn't mean to overstep."

I respond with a hearty chuckle. "Kissing your twenty-million-dollar lips is hardly a punishment."

"Twenty million, huh?" She purses said lips. "Those were the days."

I've been meaning to ask Leslie how much Ida is getting paid for this movie, but she wouldn't tell me, anyway. "How much is it these days?" I try.

There it is, then. The famous Ida Burton smile. She seems wholly herself again. "I'll share if you share."

"Sure." I look her in the eye. The air between us has shifted again. "Twelve."

Ida whistles through her teeth. "Ten." She pouts as though she's been hard done by and ten million dollars isn't an obscene amount of money. But it is two million less than I'm getting paid. "You win." She walks to the table and reaches for her water bottle.

"It's not a competition."

"You'd think that for ten million I'd be able to deliver my lines at rehearsal." She expels a sigh and walks to the railing of the deck and leans her back against it. The orange glow of the setting sun catches in her hair, making it look as if a fire has just started on the horizon. "To be completely honest with you, before you invited me over, I called Leslie in hysterics, asking her to get me out of this movie."

Perplexed by her admission, I walk over to her. "Why? Because of what happened this morning?"

She gives a slow nod. "It made me feel like my performance wasn't worth ten cents."

"Good thing Leslie didn't budge." I bump my shoulder into hers. "I never had any doubts about you."

"I suppose I'd better value your judgment about me for the twelve million it's worth." She flashes me that brilliant smile again.

"If anything, it's a comfort to know that even the great Ida Burton doubts herself sometimes." I turn toward her. "Was it the kiss?"

"Yes." She briefly flicks the tip of her tongue along her bottom lip. "And the whole gay movie thing, you know. It adds a different kind of stakes to the project."

"It better not bomb, what with the fees they have to pay us." I feel less like I'm operating in Ida's shadow now that I know I'm being paid more. It's petty but oh-so Hollywood. "I'm so glad you're still on board. I wouldn't want to kiss anyone else's gorgeous lips."

Ida's brow furrows and she emits a nervous chuckle.

"I'm sorry. I didn't mean anything by that," I say.

"Maybe we should get back to it." She squares her shoulders. "Minus the kiss. I'll try to remember."

I don't tell her that I didn't mind the kiss all that much. We're both professional actors getting paid exorbitant amounts of money for this. Although, on a movie set, a kiss is usually part of a carefully orchestrated choreography, and that was hardly the case with what happened earlier. But *A New Day* is a rom-com with a grand total of two kissing scenes and one fade to black intimate scene of our characters in bed, which doesn't even require an on-set intimacy coordinator. I haven't requested one and I would have known by now if Ida had.

"At least we know Mindy and Veronica have chemistry," I say, as I assume my position.

"They've been best friends forever," Ida says.

"That might be so, but they've never kissed before." I wink at Ida and I think I detect a faint blush on her cheeks in response, but I can't be absolutely certain.

We go through the scene a few more times, our lips not even coming close to touching again.

"We'll blow Tamara's mind at rehearsals tomorrow," I say, after we've sat again and are staring into the ocean.

"Thanks again for doing this." Ida keeps looking straight ahead. "Then again, you're clearly the lead in this movie, so it's all on you."

From the corner of my eye, I can see she's smiling.

"If it will make you feel any better, I'll happily give you a million. Just so we're even." I was planning on giving away a good percentage of what I'm getting paid to an LGBTQI+ charity.

Ida giggles. "This conversation is simply obscene."

"I totally recognize my privilege, and yes, we are grossly overpaid for what we do, but what are we meant to do? Not accept the money offered?"

"And it's not as if it doesn't come at a price," Ida muses.

"How do you mean?"

"Our personal lives." Her voice croaks a little. "How many happy long-term Hollywood couples do you know?"

"A few, I guess. Usually only one of them is in the limelight. It's like a relationship can rarely stand two stars."

"You were in a long-term thing with Brian Walsh." She looks at me now. "You don't have to tell me what happened. An image of the two of you just popped into my head out of nowhere."

"It's, uh, not a story for a beautiful night like this one."

"That bad?" Her voice is all gentleness.

"Sorry, Ida, but I really don't want to go there right now."

"Oh, no, of course. I wasn't implying that you should." She exhales deeply. "I should go, but that sunset is to die for."

"Stay," I say. "It's just me here. You're not keeping me from anything."

"I'll try not to kiss you again." Her joke takes me by surprise. Followed up by her full-wattage smile, it makes me feel strangely sorry that rehearsals will be smooch-free tomorrow.

CHAPTER EIGHT

IDA

By the time production starts two weeks later, that impromptu kiss I pressed onto Faye's lips, which wasn't even a real kiss, has grown to enormous proportions in my head. I have examined it from every possible angle and torn apart every possible motive I could have had for being so brazen as to touch my lips to hers unbidden. While there are fair arguments to be made for me being in character, I know, in my heart, there was more to it than that.

Spending the better part of the past two weeks in her company hasn't helped with erasing that special moment from my mind. And the prospect of whiling away hours and hours with each other during endless on-set waits fills me with a glee that is the opposite of what I felt on that day I froze during rehearsals.

Every evening when the assistant director gives me the sides for the next day, I read them with bated breath to see if the kissing scene is on the schedule yet. I'm guessing Tamara's waiting until we're further into the shoot before setting up more intimate takes.

Faye and I have one more scene to shoot today. As usual, we find ourselves sitting side by side in makeup as we wait to be called. I see her reflection in the mirror. She has her eyes closed as Janet does something to the skin around her eyes—probably masking her crow's feet.

My previous male co-stars only needed a flick of the makeup brush—Hollywood is more forgiving of 'character lines' in male actors. Seeing Faye go through the same rituals as me has added a level of comfort. No double standards. To be treated as complete equals. With her by my side, the energy on set is different than if she were a male actor. Or maybe that's just all in my head.

Maybe I'm just elated that, for once, I can feel a little bit closer to myself, even though I'm still pretending, even though I'm still hiding something very important. But working on this movie, where so many crew members are out and proud, has gotten under my skin in a good way. It has shown me what's possible. It has done on a microscale what this movie might do on a much bigger scale once it releases and it feels amazing to be part of this. I'm so glad I didn't pull out during rehearsals. Because I need to be around these people. I need this movie to give me the strength to see this through. To reveal my true self to the world. To do the very thing I used to deem not important, a side note, something to be ashamed of, whereas it's the opposite of all those things.

"Earth to Ida. Earth to Ida." I must have spaced out, carried away on my big coming out fantasy. "I'm just going to retouch your hair and you'll be good to go," Janet says.

In the reflection of the mirror, Faye winks at me. I return her gesture with a quick smile. Some people are lucky enough to have been given the kind of face you can't help but look at, you can't help but lose yourself in a little. A face made for the screen. Faye Fleming has one of those faces. There's an openness to it that's irresistible. That makes you want to look at it again and again. My smile widens as I look at her.

"Tomorrow's sides are in." I was so wrapped up in studying Faye's face that I didn't see Mark approach. He waves a small stack of papers in front of his face, as though fanning himself. "And, oh mama, they are H.O.T."

"Let me see." I reach out my hand.

"Where are mine?" Faye asks Mark.

"You know Brandon. Always one step behind the best in the biz." He bats his lashes.

I ignore their banter. Could this be it? I skim through the pages for tomorrow's scenes. My heart starts beating double time. I've repeated those lines a million times in my head by now.

Brandon joins us and gives Faye the script. She flicks through it.

"Looks like smooch-time tomorrow," Faye says, finding my gaze in the mirror. Behind me, Janet is touching up my hair, making it stand out as wide as it will go.

"Time, please, ladies," Joey, the assistant director sticks her head around the corner.

I'm already so consumed with tomorrow's scenes that I've forgotten what we're meant to play right now. Oh yes, the scene where Veronica and Mindy arrive at the wedding together, right before a lot of confusion and innuendo ensues.

"Good to go," Janet says.

As we walk to the soundstage, I whisper in Mark's ear, "Make sure Faye sticks around after we wrap. I need to talk to her about something."

"On it, boss." Mark gives me a thumbs-up.

We finish the wedding arrival scene in three takes. As soon as Tamara calls it a wrap for the day, I hurry after Faye, who's headed back to makeup to get her face cleaned. I follow her, but I have to be patient. Although there's nothing wrong with one actor asking the other to her house to go over tomorrow's scenes, I don't want an audience. That's decades of living in the closet for you. My patience is vast. My paranoia always amped all the way up.

Faye and I get our makeup removed. My face seems to take a bit longer and Faye's already getting up. I try to find her gaze in the mirror, but she seems suddenly in a hurry.

"Janet, could we have a minute, please?"

"I'll be done with you in ten seconds," Janet says.

I'm not sure I have ten seconds, but surely Faye will stop by her trailer before leaving. And I have Mark trying to stall her as well.

Janet's ten seconds feel like ten minutes. I quickly thank her and rush to Faye's trailer. The door is open, and I spot Joey inside.

"Ah, Ida," Joey says. "If you have any questions or want to discuss anything at all about tomorrow's scene, call me any time. Even if it's at three in the morning. Tamara wants you both to feel super comfortable about it. There will be extra time for rehearsal, if needed, to create the right kind of vibe."

"I think we'll be fine," Faye says.

"It's great that it all worked out in rehearsal, but this time around, we need an actual kiss on camera," Joey says.

"Surely you wouldn't be making such a big deal out of this if it were a male and female character kissing?" Faye sounds amused.

"Hey, I'm just saying." Joey holds up her hands. "If you need any tips on the art of women kissing women, I'm your gal. Okay?"

I chuckle nervously. This set is full of lesbians, all with supposed gaydar, yet none of them have picked up anything about me? I guess I won those four Oscars for a reason.

"You're going to show us how it's done?" Faye asks, her voice a fountain of glee. "Who will you kiss?"

"Who would you like me to kiss?" Joey arches up her eyebrows. "Just for the record, I'd kiss you two any day of the week, any hour of the day."

"I think we've got it, Joey," Faye says, rolling her eyes.

"It's not the same as kissing a guy." Joey starts to make her way out.

I make room for her to leave. I turn my face away for fear I might be caught blushing. Goodness, how different it is.

"I want you to be properly prepared," Joey adds.

"If I didn't know you to be such a professional, I would suspect you of getting a real kick out of this conversation," Faye says.

"I'm just living the dream, Faye." She holds up a hand to signal her goodbye. "I'm serious. Call me any time."

I linger in the trailer's doorway, chuckling along with Faye for an instant. "Can I come in?"

Faye nods. I close the door behind me.

"Nervous about tomorrow?" Faye asks.

"Yeah." I draw a breath hoping it will give me extra

courage. "About that, um, do you think we need to… prepare more?"

"More kissing practice?" Faye starts unbuttoning her blouse.

I don't know where to look. "Yes," I manage to say with fully averted gaze.

She lets the blouse slide off her shoulders and drapes it over a hanger. For heaven's sake. This doesn't look good. I can't ask her to come over to my house for some kissing while she's half undressed.

"I'll wait for you outside." I start for the door.

"Jesus, Ida, we'll be kissing each other tomorrow. You can see me in my bra. Don't worry, I'm not taking that off." I hear some rustling. "There. You can feast your eyes on me again." She's slipped a T-shirt over her head. I hope she doesn't start on her pants next.

"Um." I feel like the first time I went to an audition. Inadequate. Tripping over every single word. Certain my acting career would never work out, but holding onto the tiniest strand of belief regardless because I wanted it so much. "So, you want to hook up tonight?" Instantly, my cheeks are on fire. "I'm sorry." I deploy my most self-deprecating laugh to erase my slip of the tongue.

"Hook up?" Faye throws her head back in laughter. I guess even the notion is utterly hilarious. Why wouldn't it be to her? "Damn, we're suddenly moving fast."

"Meet up," I say. "Long day."

"Sure. Why not?"

"Thanks." I hurry out of her trailer before I die of mortification.

"Hey, Ida." Faye yells behind me. "Your place or mine?"

A few heads turn. "Mine," I shout back.

As I head to my trailer, I pretend I'm the straightest person in the world and I've just scored a date with the most masculine man in Hollywood—Brian Walsh springs to mind. It has worked for me well enough in the past and it's only about ten steps until I close the door behind me and breathe.

CHAPTER NINE

FAYE

When I show up at Ida's, she looks so glamorous, so subtly but efficiently made up, it's as though Janet just had her skilled hands all over her. Ida's wide-legged slacks are so crisp and her silk blouse so wrinkle-free, it makes me suspect she has a wardrobe department hidden somewhere in her house in the hills. The things I've seen people do with their money in this town, anything's possible.

I feel a bit frumpy in my jeans and cotton shirt, but I didn't know this was anything more than some impromptu rehearsing for tomorrow.

"Going anywhere fancy after?" I ask as she escorts me into her house.

"What? No."

"You look like ten million bucks."

"Ten exactly?" Her lips go wide into that famous smile. "That's what I was going for."

"I'm not paying you any of that money so no need to go to any trouble on my account." She might not be dressed up like this for me, of course. Silly me for assuming. "You must have had a hot dinner date before I arrived."

Ida shakes her head. "I wish, but your arrival is the one and only highlight of my evening."

She leads me to a lounge with cream-colored couches, a large rug of the same color, and a low glass table. The previous time I came here, I barely noticed the decor of her house. I was still too starstruck to notice anything but Ida. I'm over all of that now. We're just two co-workers getting together—albeit two co-workers who have to kiss each other on the lips.

As she grabs us a couple of bottles of water, I look around her house. Above the faux fireplace, there's a large wedding picture of her and Derek, which strikes me as odd. In fact, this whole place feels a bit odd. Like it's not really lived in. Like it's a movie set more than someone's home. Maybe Ida has a place somewhere else, or a few, where she spends most of her time.

"You and Derek must really have parted on good terms." I point at the wedding picture.

"Yes," is all Ida says, clearly unwilling to broach the subject, so I don't push. The other day, while waiting in my trailer, I googled specifically for stories about Ida and Derek's divorce, but apart from the big revelation that Derek turned out to be gay, there wasn't all that much to find. Another odd thing.

When Brian and I split, every last detail the press could find was smeared all over the front pages for months on end —all but the one thing that had brought us down. Ida isn't the only one with an excellent publicist.

"Do you want to get started right away with the scene?" I ask.

"I didn't mean to be short with you about that picture. I have my reasons for keeping it up there. I'm just... I mean, I really like you, Faye. I very much enjoy working with you. It's been a real treat so far, but you know what decades in this business does to you. It's not easy for me to talk about certain things."

"Oh, totally. I get it." Of course I do.

"Maybe we can talk for a bit before we start... kissing." She rubs her palms on her fancy slacks. "The reason I may come across as extra nervous is that I haven't done a kissing scene in quite some time. It's not something I've ever particularly enjoyed, what with having a close-up camera jammed in your face, and a bunch of people crowding in when you're trying to make something appear very intimate while the situation is the exact opposite."

"Yeah. I get it." I scoff. "In my last movie, I kissed both Danny White and Mario Velez and it's not as if it was horrible, but it's just... it somehow always manages to feel kind of too invasive. I actually prefer a tightly choreographed love scene over a kissing scene. The vibe is different."

"Which movie was that?" Ida's shuffling anxiously in her seat.

"*Twice Bitten, Once Shy*. It's coming out in a few months. I'm starting the whole promo shindig after we finish shooting *A New Day*." I shrug. "But I don't want to make too big a deal out of this, either. We don't want to be in our heads about it too much. That will not have the desired effect."

Ida nods. "It does tend to get extra awkward after a few takes."

"Let's go for the one-take kiss."

"That will require a lot of practice tonight."

"We've already done it perfectly before. Maybe this particular scene is why we do what we do. Maybe it's the scene that will define the rest of our careers."

"Way to keep the pressure off."

"You're right. I'm sorry." I glance at her. "I don't think either one of us has anything left to prove."

"Really?" She pulls down the corners of her mouth. "That's not how I feel about it. After the divorce, I took a kind of involuntary break. I didn't want to, but I felt like I had to. Afterward, it wasn't exactly difficult to get good parts, but none of the movies I've done in the past few years have made any significant impact at the box office. And, well, sometimes I can't help but feel like I've lost some of my old magic. The thing that made any Ida Burton movie an event. No questions asked. Not that every single one of those movies was good. I cringe at some of them." She rolls her eyes. "The sheer misogyny and the bad sexist jokes in some of my old movies." She pretends to shudder. "Some of that stuff is pretty horrible now. That's why this movie in particular is a big deal for me. And, of course, all eyes are going to be on that kiss. And that's why I feel I have a lot to prove."

I swivel my body and rest my knee on the couch. "But still, Ida, in the end, it's just a movie. The worst that can happen is that it bombs. In that case, we move on to greener pastures."

She shakes her head vehemently. "The worst that can happen is it gets panned by the critics. That you and I get blamed for not having enough chemistry, because it's supposed to be one of the main ingredients of this film." She pauses. "Maybe it's different for you. The last ten years have been really amazing for you. You've cleaned up at every award show, stacking your shelves with little golden stat-uettes. You have far less to prove. If anything, this movie is like an in-between snack for you."

"It's really not. I'm taking this movie very seriously."

"Still, it would be easy enough to brush off as a hit-and-miss project for you. I don't think I could do that."

"Ida, come on. That's not how I've approached any movie I've ever done. Not even when I was starting out."

"I didn't mean to imply that. Sorry. I expressed myself clumsily." She exhales slowly. "It's just my insecurities acting up. Sometimes it's hard not to feel like I'm over the hill. Like the best of my career is behind me."

I shuffle closer to her in the couch. I can't believe I have to be the one to tell Ida Burton that she will never lose her luster. That she can still light up any movie set just by simply walking onto it. That she will always draw a crowd no matter what she does. And that she looks fabulous and sexy and like one of the biggest movie stars Hollywood has ever produced. In fact, I don't think I will be the one to tell her that.

I put a hand on her arm and give her a gentle squeeze. "All of this because you have to kiss a woman on screen?" I decide a joke is better in the circumstances.

She erupts into a kind of choked chuckle. "Oh, Faye, you have no idea."

She's right. I don't. Although I do have a pretty good idea of the doubts going through any actor's mind when faced with an intimate scene. "Put all of those emotions into that kiss and you'll blow everyone's mind."

"There's an idea." There's a lightness to her tone again. "You'd think we're professional actors who have a clue of what they're doing."

"Shall we, then?"

"Let's get to it." She briefly looks at my hand on her arm. "You're getting handsy already."

I give her arm another quick squeeze before letting go. Then I get up. "I hope you're off-book."

"It's a kiss," Ida says. "I usually don't need a script for that."

CHAPTER TEN

IDA

Can Faye hear the pounding of my heart? It slams against my ribcage with such fury, I'm afraid its foolish antics might be visible to the naked eye. But Faye just stands there, waiting for me to deliver my lines—the ones leading up to our kiss. At least, this time, she's expecting it.

We recite our lines and then I lean in. Am I acting? And if I'm not, is that some sort of violation? A brazen breach of boundaries? I don't much care as her gentle, flowery scent overtakes my nostrils and her lips part a fraction for me. We're not supposed to touch each other while we kiss, only our lips briefly press together, after which our characters break apart, one much more mortified than the other.

Acting or not, Faye's lips are impossibly soft against mine, and being so close to her makes the entire expanse of my skin tingle. Until we have to break away—much too soon for my liking. But this is kissing practice, which means we get to do it again. I deliver my lines and lean in again, but her lips are not where I expect them to be.

I pull back and examine her face. It's possible that I was being a bit too intense. My house is absent of on-set energy. It's just the two of us under some soft lighting. "Are you okay?" I'd best be the one to ask first.

"Yeah." Faye steps back. "Part of me thinks we've got this."

"Oh." Her enthusiasm for practice is understandably not as boundless as mine. "Yes. Sure."

"It's not the most elaborate of kisses." Is her voice a bit husky? It's probably my imagination. "There's really nothing complicated about it."

I suck my bottom lip between my teeth and nod. I don't know how I can safely find out if that's the real reason why we're stopping before we've even got started. It's impossible for me to discern it from the context because this situation is highly unusual. Chances are I screwed up somehow, though. But I can't just come out—no pun intended—and ask her.

"Maybe one more time," Faye says, tapping a painted fingernail against her chin, as though this requires great thought—as though we're engaging in the most complex bout of method acting ever.

"Whatever you want."

She arches up one perfectly plucked eyebrow. "Really?"

"Uh-huh."

"Big words coming from the likes of you, Ida." She throws in some girlish charm. "Come here." She moves her fingers in a come-hither-kind-of-way and I almost swoon. Clearly, there's so much more going on here for me than for her, because I'm a frustrated, closeted lesbian kissing the most gorgeous woman. But is there more to it than that? Maybe I've been too afraid to consider it. Maybe I haven't wanted to admit my attraction to Faye Fleming because denying myself such an indulgence is like second nature to me. For that reason, even if I am attracted to her—and the evidence is piling up—I know that it will pass. I know this better than I know anything else because it's the story of my life. Instead of actor, it should say battler-extraordinaire of temptation at the top of my resume.

I step closer to Faye and the realization that I might want more than this chaste movie kiss from her makes me feel a little awkward—like I'm fifteen years old rather than almost fifty.

The lines come out automatically now, as though they're part of us, which should make Tamara very happy tomorrow, and then, when I press my lips against hers this time around, it becomes near impossible to tear myself away from her. The kiss lasts a few moments longer than it should and when we finally break apart, I can only hope the color of my cheeks isn't the same fiery red as my hair.

"You were really into it this time, Ida." Faye eyes me suspiciously. Or maybe I'm the suspicious one. I don't know anymore. My head spins a little. My legs feel a touch wobbly.

"I—I was channeling Veronica like the ten-million-dollar actor I am," I joke lamely.

"Worth every penny," Fays says and sucks her lips between her teeth, as though wanting to erase the impression of mine from them.

When I signed up for this movie, despite my ulterior motive, I had no idea what kind of a mind-fuck it would end up being because I didn't know Faye Fleming was going to be such a delight to be around—and to kiss.

"We're definitely ready for tomorrow," I say.

Faye nods. "We have an early call time, so I think I'll go now."

I consider an even lamer joke about kissing her good-night, but instead I just nod. At this point, I want her to go so I can gather myself. Or call Derek. Or watch one of her movies. Or—

"Ida?"

"Yes." I walk her to the front door.

"Are we okay?" she asks.

"Very much so."

"I'll see you in the morning." She slants her body toward me and presses the lightest of kisses to my cheek, leaving me so dazed, I stare at the empty driveway for a good few minutes after she's gone.

Faye and I watch the second team rehearse our upcoming kiss. Our stand-ins don't actually kiss, although their lips hover very close to each other. In a way, I'm less nervous than last night. It's different, because we're not alone. Although I'm grateful for the practice we've had and I'm sure it will make the shooting go more smoothly, I tossed and turned half the night, trying to process my emotions. We're nowhere near the end of this shoot. I have a lot of time left to spend with Faye. We have another, more elaborate kissing scene coming up. Despite all the practice I've had getting over women I'm attracted to but can't possibly have, this is going to be a tough one because of the close proximity and Faye's general awesomeness. Her unexpected kindness. Her tremendous talent. Her way of making me feel at ease in some ways and getting under my skin in others.

"They've got great chemistry," Faye says about our stand-ins. "Looks like we've got big shoes to fill."

Joey sidles up to us, looking surprisingly solemn. Kissing scenes are taken very seriously on set and despite yesterday's banter, our assistant director adheres to this principle.

"We'll be good to go in five, ladies," Joey says. "If you're ready."

"We're more than ready," Faye says. "Try to keep us away from each other." She turns to me and shoots me a big fat wink. If the crew isn't going to joke about it, it's up to us to relieve the tension. But I have no comeback for Faye. I'm too busy trying to ignore those wretched butterflies in my stomach when she looks at me like that.

Once we've taken our places, Faye slaps her palm against her forehead. "Shouldn't have had that garlic dressing on my salad for lunch. Sorry."

I laugh at her attempt to inject some silliness into the situation as we wait for the *Action* call. It's easy enough to laugh with her. Most of my nerves about this have been dealt with. I'm no longer the frozen, stammering mess I was in rehearsal and I look forward to showing the crew this. I want the producers to know I'm worth the money they've paid me. That I can show up on the day and kiss another woman on the lips as if I've been doing it all my life.

"And... Action," Tamara shouts.

"It's about what I feel for you," I whisper, feeling like the best actor that has ever lived, because it's true. I don't have to act. I don't have to search for something deep inside myself to make my words sound as though they are the truest words ever uttered. I look into Faye's eyes and am met with a glimmer of something. She's a damn fine actor herself and, so often, it's all in the eyes. The close-up camera hovers near my face but it's as though it's not there. It's like it's just a bug buzzing around us while Faye and I are about to kiss. Easy enough to ignore because of all the rest that's going on around us. When I close my eyes and bridge the final distance between our lips, it's not as my character Veronica. It's as myself. And as myself, my truest, most real self, I feel how everything fades away around me, how the crew disappears, the cameras dissolve, and it's just Faye and I as my lips melt into hers.

Damn it. I did it again. I quickly pull away and act as though it was written in the script, that this kiss was meant to last several seconds instead of a mere instant.

"Cut," Tamara says. "Wow. Amazing."

Once I've drummed up the courage to look at Faye, I'm met with more than a little trepidation in her gaze.

"Your timing seemed a little off," Faye says.

"Yeah?" I respond innocently, another something I've perfected over the years.

She nods and looks at Tamara, probably for backup.

Tamara joins us and says, "Absolutely great first take. We're going to have to do that again, though." She singles me out. "Ida, um, if you could pull back just a little. Just a tiny bit. You know what I mean?"

"Yes." I know exactly what she means, but what I don't seem to know any longer is how to control my lips. They've taken on a mind of their own. They've become addicted to Faye lips—and who can blame them? "Sorry." I try to think of a joke to hide behind, but I can't think of any. All I can think of is kissing Faye again. Of how I don't want the kiss to stop. Of how I want to pull her near and let my lips… *Stop it, Ida.* "Got it."

Tamara asks the crew to set up the shot again. Faye and I take a seat in our designated chairs while we wait.

"I'm sorry, Faye. I know we were aiming for a single take."

"I think we both know that was an illusion. When was the last time you shot a scene in a single take?"

I shrug. I'm not sure I ever have. Janet comes over to check our hair and makeup.

"Maybe you should count to one," Faye says after Janet has left. She looks at me with eyebrows arched all the way up. "Do you think you can manage that? As soon as our lips touch, you just go 'one' in your head, and then pull back."

I'm glad she finds this funny. I really am. She's a good sport, which doesn't help with my desire to kiss her for much longer than the count of one.

"It must be your lips. I think Janet might have applied some glue-like substance instead of lipstick."

"Oh, sure." There's a smile in Faye's voice. "It must be that." She dabs her lip with her fingertip. "Big error in the makeup department. We should get her fired. I'd feel really bad for such a lovely lady to lose her job, but if it needs to be done…" Faye pins her gaze on me, delicious lips pursed.

While we banter back and forth, I come up with my game plan for the next take. Instead of focusing on Faye's lips and on how divine it is to be able to kiss them, to be so close to her, to feel this rush of energy through my veins that makes me feel more alive than I have in years, I'll think of one of the worst moments of my career. The day my carefully crafted charade with Derek fell apart and he decided he'd had enough of not being himself. The fear of being outed as a by-product of his decision paralyzed me for years.

It stopped me from taking on challenging and rewarding projects. It kept me from giving the kind of performances I knew I could give. Because even when you can hide behind a fictional character, you always have to give a part of yourself that's real. You always have to leave a little something, a minute fraction of your soul, out there, for your performance to really connect with the audience.

That's the real reason I haven't had a box office smash in so long. Because I haven't been able to play a character that hit a nerve with the audience.

"Ready for take two?" Joey asks.

Faye and I take our places. We say our lines. I lean in and kiss her the way I'm meant to. Passionate but brief. Full of partially restrained desire. As it turns out, I don't have to turn my mind elsewhere. I don't have to conjure up the moment when I sent out that post-divorce statement. Because as much as I want to kiss Faye for much longer than the count of one, I'm not allowed to.

CHAPTER ELEVEN
FAYE

On the way to my trailer, I hear Charlie's voice close by. I don't see her but I hear her mention Ida. I stop in my tracks and listen.

"Maybe those rumors are true," another voice says.

"Come on, Liz," Charlie says. "If there were even a grain of truth to it, we of all people would know."

What rumors are they referring to? I slip into the tight space between two trailers and inch closer to where they're having this conversation. Curiosity is getting the better of my sense of decorum.

"Why would we? Just because we're lesbians?"

No news there. Both Charlie and Liz are so out, a closet is just something you keep clothes in for them.

"Maybe she's bi," Liz says.

"If she's anything but straight as an arrow, she's done an amazing job keeping it under wraps."

"Until the day she had to kiss Faye Fleming." A frisson runs up my spine at the mention of my name. I know I shouldn't be eavesdropping on Charlie and Liz, but I can't for the life of me pull myself away from overhearing this. They are talking about me now as well, after all.

"That would be tempting for anyone," Charlie says.

I can't believe what I'm hearing. I've known Charlie for years.

"What?" Charlie sounds as though Liz has just looked at her in a very questioning way. I tiptoe closer to the end of the makeshift corridor I'm hiding in. I'd love to see their faces as well as hear their words.

"She does have a very kissable quality about her," Liz says.

My heart does a strange pitter-patter in my chest as I stick my head out from behind the corner. Christ. I hope no one can see me—how utterly ludicrous I would look. Instead of focusing on that, I focus on the conversation again. Are they being serious or just chatting? Killing time between takes? On set, acting is only a tiny portion of any shooting day. Waiting can be long. Things get said. So many romances ignite on set because they are given all the time and space in the world to do so. That's how it all started with me and Brian.

I've missed the next part of their conversation due to my shuffling around. I try to stand stock-still, holding my breath. It makes my heart beat even more furiously in my throat.

"She did have a gay husband," Charlie says. They're back on Ida then.

"Have you gotten any vibes off her?" Liz asks. "Has she made the old gaydar ping?"

"Not in the slightest."

"Some people are so deep in the closet, it becomes like Stockholm Syndrome," Liz says.

Charlie chuckles.

"It's not funny." Liz sounds serious. I try to peek around the corner a bit farther. They're sitting with their backs to me only a few yards away. "It's sad if that's how you have to live your life."

"Sorry, but if Ida Burton's a deeply closeted lesbian, that's nothing but her own choice," Charlie says.

I can't believe what I'm hearing. I know they're only speculating—gossiping, really—but what if it's true? Why did Ida's kiss linger? Not just on set today, but last night at her house as well. And why on earth did she have that wedding picture of her and Derek so prominently featured in her living room and hardly anything else? Why has she been so notoriously single since her divorce? But if Ida were in the closet—and it's still the biggest of ifs—why would she do this movie? Why would she jeopardize what she's managed to hide for so long for a movie part?

"There you are," a whisper comes from behind, making me jump out of my skin.

I turn around and look into Brandon's stunned face.

"What are you doing skulking between two trailers?" he whispers.

I bring a finger to my lips, indicating he should remain quiet. But I can't stand around here any longer listening to this. Moreover, I don't want Brandon to get wind of what they're saying about Ida. He might end up asking Mark about it, who might tell Ida, and then what? I study Brandon's face and consider this plan, but I'm not going to be using my assistant to get to the bottom of this.

"Just stretching my legs," I whisper back. "Nothing for you to worry about."

Brandon wasn't born yesterday and he gives me a look,

but he doesn't quiz me further—I am still his boss—nor does he demand to see what's going on behind the corner. I gesticulate for him to move back and we exit my hiding place.

"Mark asked me to tell you that Ida would like to speak to you whenever suits you," Brandon says.

"Good." Brandon walks me to my trailer. "I would like to speak to her as well."

"About that kiss?" he asks. "The set's abuzz with rumors." He's right about that. I just hope, for Ida's sake, that other people aren't having the same conversation as Charlie and Liz.

I don't respond to Brandon because I don't want to give any rumors more oxygen to spread. Instead of going inside my trailer, I find Ida's.

"You called for me?" I say after Mark has let me into Ida's trailer.

"Can you give us a minute, Mark?"

Mark leaves us and closes the door behind him.

"Look—" Ida starts.

"Are you—" I say at the same time.

"Please, sit." She makes room on the three-seater couch and positions herself at the far end. "Drink?"

"I'm fine." I sit beside her. "Are you all right, Ida?"

"Sure. Why do you ask?" Even when she narrows her eyes like that, something about her sparkles. She probably gets out of bed in the morning radiating glossiness and that undefinable X factor.

"No reason. You wanted to talk?" I figure I'd better hear

what she has to say before I tell her what I've heard. I do think she should know what's being said about her.

"I wanted to apologize for earlier. I could have been more professional. I mean, I should have been, after all the practicing we've been doing."

After hearing Charlie and Liz's conversation, I feel like I need to second-guess everything. I invited Ida over to my house to rehearse that kiss. I let her kiss me in the dusk with the ocean roaring in the background. Did I send some sort of message that she could have misconstrued?

"I think you know that you don't have to apologize to me. I know how these things can go. Acting is a vulnerable process. You lost yourself in the character's journey. If you ask me, that's supposed to be a good thing. Not something to apologize for." What am I babbling about? I'm nervous about what I really want to tell her.

"Thanks for being so understanding. Not everyone would be." The smile she sends me is one with dimmed wattage.

"Look, Ida, there's something you should know. Something I heard being whispered about on set."

"Okay." Ida sits up a bit straighter.

I should have thought this through more before barging in here, albeit on invitation. "Charlie and Liz, um, just now, outside, I heard them debate your... um, sexual orientation."

"What?" Despite the fierceness of her voice, a rigid stillness comes over her.

"It's just talk, you know." I try to make my voice sound light. If Brandon were here, he would berate me for making a big deal out of this. "But I figured you'd want to know what's being said about you."

"W-what did they say?"

"They were referring to rumors about you and wondering whether they might be true."

"Rumors that I might be a… lesbian?" She almost whispers the last word.

I nod.

"Jesus Christ." She bounces her foot up and down. "It's because of that wretched kiss."

And so it always all comes back to the kiss. I'm the other person in the scene with her. I'm the one kissing her back. Yet, for me, it's just a job. It's not something I've had any problem with. It seems to be very different for Ida.

"About that kiss." I try to find her gaze, but she doesn't let me. "I get that it's not an everyday thing, but is there a reason why it's been so difficult for you?"

"What?" She huffs out some air through her nostrils, like a bull about to attack a red rag. "No, of course not. I don't know where those rumors are coming from, but you can be sure that I'll be setting Charlie and Liz straight about them." She wrings her hands together. "It's not true. What they're saying. It's bullshit." Her face has gone pale and she seems to be purposefully avoiding my gaze.

"Okay." This must be the worst performance Ida Burton has ever given in her life, but it's not up to me to contradict her. I'm just her co-star. We have a budding friendship—and a few movie kisses—between us, but that's it.

"Just, please don't tell anyone about this," Ida urges me.

"Ida, um…" Because of the movie we're working on, I feel like I should say something. "I just want you to know that even if it were true, that would also be perfectly fine."

She shoots out of her seat and starts pacing, but the trailer isn't very big, and she has nowhere to go.

"It's not true. Okay?" Her voice is full of defensive aggression now.

Ida's hostile reaction doesn't faze me because I feel sorry for her. In front of me, agony contorting her face, stands one of the world's best actors, one of the most successful women on the planet, and she's about to fall apart because she doesn't believe she can be her true self.

"Ida." I slowly rise. I don't want to antagonize her more. She radiates the energy of a caged animal. Maybe that's how she feels inside. "It's okay."

"Please, leave," she says, her voice snagging in her throat.

I don't believe there's much point in me staying with her when she's in this state.

"You know where to find me if you want to talk." Before I open the door, I say, "I'm here for you."

Her eyes blaze with a different kind of fire and if looks could kill, I'd be burnt toast by now.

CHAPTER TWELVE

IDA

I lean against the closed door Faye just walked out of. I take a few deep breaths to steady myself. To remind myself this is what I wanted. Not what just happened exactly, but something like this. An event to force me out of the closet. Something to break the spiral of fear I've been trapped in all my life. Because I've had enough of all this pretending. Of fulfilling studio bosses' and moviegoers' straight fantasies about me. Of keeping all these feelings tucked deep inside and wishing they would just go away. It's not working anymore. It has never worked, even though I've been excellent at telling myself that it has.

Just a little while longer. Just a few more millions in the bank. One more movie. One more year of loneliness on top of all the time I've spent loathing myself for who I am.

I inhale deeply and let the air flow out through my nose slowly. I push back a tear that threatens to spill out of the corner of my eye. This is no time to cry.

This is the time to tell someone. Just one person. To let someone in. To share something of myself with them that I thought I could push away into oblivion, despite knowing better.

That person can only be Faye.

Mark is hovering outside my trailer. Thank goodness Tamara saved the kissing scene for last and we've wrapped for the day.

I walk over to Faye's trailer and knock on the door. While I wait for her to answer, I see Charlie walking to the break room. I'm not going to call her out on what she's been saying about me. What could that possibly achieve?

Before I enter, I ask Mark to not let anyone disturb us. Faye's alone. There's no sign of Brandon.

I wish I didn't have to do this in this trailer, but, in a way, it's appropriate. I've spent more waking hours in movie set trailers than I have in my own home. This is where I live most of my life. In makeshift rooms, in small spaces, the tightness of which has never made it easier to contain my feelings. On the contrary.

"Hey," Faye's voice is soft. "Sit with me." She pats the couch, but I'm not sure I should sit so close to her. Then I shake off my instinct. I haven't come here to declare my undying love for Faye Fleming. That's not what this is about —nor am I in love with her.

I walk over to her and sit. Before I speak, I glance at her kind face, her soft gaze, her inviting smile. Even Derek has admitted that Faye has that thing for which millions of women would kill. That elusive attractive quality that probably amounts to a certain symmetry in her face. How the tip of her nose perks upward and those two lone freckles on her cheekbone draw the eye and make it impossible to look away.

"The most commercial face in Hollywood," Leslie called Faye once. "After yours, obviously, darling."

"You probably know why I'm here." My voice is surprisingly steady. It does not reflect how I feel. A drop of sweat trickles down my spine. The back of my neck feels damp where my hair falls against it. I push a tangle of curls behind my ears, where it doesn't stay. It never does.

"Tell me."

"I don't even know how to say this. I never have. I—"

"Try, Ida. Try for me, please."

I swallow hard, like I need to clear my throat before I say the words that millions of people have said before me. That none of us should still be required to say. That this town, this industry that revolves around money and image and status much more than around happiness and love, has forced me into keeping to myself.

"I... I like women." There. Easy as pie. "I always have." The first small wave of relief washes over me. "My marriage to Derek was one big sham. Something that worked out well for both of us at the time, until it didn't. Until he broke free of it and I didn't." I chuckle at the obviousness of my statement. "I've always chosen to remain in the closet for my career and for the longest time I managed to be okay with that, because it's just what you do in Hollywood." I shake my head because it sounds so utterly ridiculous but it's also the simple yet brutal truth. "I'm far from the only one. But now, I'm no longer okay with it."

Faye inhales sharply. She sends me an encouraging nod. "I'm so sorry, Ida."

"Don't be. It was my choice. I didn't have to do it, but I did. Until now."

"You hid it for good reason."

"That's debatable." Is money a good reason? Is fame?

"I can't imagine how hard it's been for you," Faye says. "And how hard it was to come out just now. Thanks for telling me."

"I kissed you." I try a tight-lipped smile. "I couldn't lie to you much longer." I hope she knows I'm joking.

"About that…" Faye cocks her head. "Yes, you did indeed kind of kiss me."

"Sort of, but not really." Perhaps only I will ever know that's a flagrant lie.

"Are you saying you didn't want to kiss me?" This is Faye Fleming. She's not intimidated by me in the least.

"I was required to kiss you, for the movie."

"Is that why you took this part? Because you knew you'd be playing opposite me and you'd get to kiss me?"

"No."

"Oh." I'm good enough at my job to see she's putting on an over-the-top act. "Serves me right. Thinking it was all about me."

"Look, Faye, all jokes aside… I will need this to stay between us for now."

"That goes without saying." She regards me intently. "Nobody knows, apart from Derek?"

"Some people do. People I've… had dalliances with. But there haven't been many. I always considered it too risky. It's hard to be discreet in this town."

"You just made it look easy."

"It was far from easy. I've…" But I don't want a pity party from Faye. Besides, by her own admission, she hasn't had that easy a time of it in the relationship department. I shrug. "I'm not that old. I reckon it's not too late for me yet."

"You can say that again." Faye nods at the door. "If you

go out on that set and announce you're ready to be loved by a woman, you'll be married by the time this movie's done shooting."

I chuckle heartily. In the absence of love, often humor is the only thing that has kept me going.

"You're not mad I'm doing this movie for other reasons as well?"

Faye shakes her head. "What's your master plan? Do you have a big coming out moment planned?"

"There isn't a grand master plan, I just… I went with my gut on this one. I instinctively knew I had to do this movie. That it was now or never, so to speak."

"You're lucky I didn't swat you away when your lips lingered too long."

"Hey, you invited me over for kissing practice."

Faye erupts into laughter. "Right. This is all on me."

"No, thank you for being so… understanding and kind." This might be construed as blatant flirting, but I don't care. I really want to say this to Faye. "Why a catch like yourself is single beats me, Faye. You're the full package."

She sends me a dazzling smile—one that could easily rival my own when I'm at the top of my game. "I'm just as flawed as the next person, but thank you. I appreciate the great Ida Burton seeing me that way."

I return her smile. There's nothing tight about it any longer. I haven't just told another person my biggest secret; I've also made a new friend. As for my budding feelings for her, nothing has changed. I'll still have to deploy all the experience I've built up over the years to curb them.

CHAPTER THIRTEEN

FAYE

"Can you believe that Mark acts as though he's so much better than me just because he's Ida Burton's assistant?" Brandon says. "Like she's somehow higher in the Hollywood hierarchy than you." He clicks his tongue as though that is the most ridiculous thing he's ever had to consider.

I so wish I could share with him what Ida told me. He's a flamboyant loudmouth with high ambitions of his own, but beneath all his glittery bravado, he has a heart of gold. A heart that goes out to kids who have been kicked out by their parents, which is why he spends some of his precious free time working at an LGBTQI+ helpline and volunteering at a shelter in West Hollywood. I try to do my bit by writing checks every few months, as if money can ever replace the acceptance of a loving parent.

If anyone would understand Ida's plight, it's Brandon, but a promise is a promise and I can't break the one I made to Ida. What I can do is stop by Ava and Charlie's and confront Charlie with what she and Liz were whispering about on set.

"Are you sure whatever it was the two of you had going is fully over?" I ask Brandon.

"Oh yes. Mark's got this 'amazing' boyfriend who wants to marry him."

"Mark's about ten years older than you. He's in a different place."

"Thanks, darling." Brandon beams me a smile. "He's actually only five years older than me, but he does make it look as though it's ten."

The car comes to a stop.

"This is you. See you tomorrow," I say, happy to have propped up his ego.

"Have a good night." Brandon air kisses me and shoots me a big wink before getting out of the car.

On the way to Malibu, I text Ava to see if she's home. She texts me back to say she's on set all evening. Although it's not my habit, I suppose I could text Charlie directly. We are working together. This movie wouldn't even exist if it weren't for Charlie Cross. Ida would still be firmly in the closet if it weren't for Charlie as well.

I text her to ask if she'll be home tonight. Instead of texting me back, she calls me.

"Is everything okay?" Charlie asks. "Are you having second thoughts about today's shoot?"

"No, Charlie," I reassure her. "Everything's fine, but I wanted to ask you something. I'll be in Malibu in about thirty minutes. Can I stop by yours?"

"I'm still at work. How about I drop by yours in an hour?"

"That works for me."

"You're sure there's nothing I need to worry about?"

"Nope." This must be driving her a little crazy, but she deserves it after her bout of on-set gossip—not that I've never been guilty of engaging in some of that. But this is different. Ida clearly feels her reputation is on the line somehow. She must feel very strongly about it if she's kept such a vital part of herself hidden for so long. "See you in a bit."

I end the call and contemplate Ida's years at the very top of the Hollywood food chain, when she and Derek were married and lit up the red carpet holding each other's hand, pretending to be something they were not. This town is built on make-believe and I understand Ida's decision to hide all too well. But why didn't she just come out when Derek did? His career did suffer, but so did hers, even though she remained in the closet.

My phone rings. Ava's name appears on the screen.

"Charlie's worried you're going to get her fired from her own movie," Ava says, without bothering with hello.

I roll my eyes. I'm sure it helps Charlie greatly in her work, but her dramatic streak is as problematic as it is legendary. "Oh, please. Why would I want Charlie fired? I love this movie. I love the script. I want Charlie to remain exactly where she is, coming up with line after wonderful line for my character to deliver."

"She's worried it's about the scene you shot today."

"Jesus, Ava, what is this?"

"I know. It's like she called her mom, and her mom needs to call the principal." She bursts into a chuckle. "Ever since rehearsals, Charlie's been nervous about the scene where you and Ida's character kiss. How did it go?"

"If you've spoken to Charlie, you know it went absolutely fine." I realize this conversation might be held against me at some point, if Ida does come out. "Ida and I are both professionals to the core."

"Okay." There's a muffled sound on the other end of the line. "Sorry. They're calling me to the set. I have to go."

On the remainder of the drive, I consider that Ava's career didn't suffer from her coming out at all. I guess it can go either way. And Ava isn't an actor. There are so many factors. I count my lucky stars that coming out is something I've never had to consider.

"Look, Charlie," I cut to the chase. "I overheard you and Liz gossiping on set today."

Her blue eyes grow a touch wider. "Ab-about what?"

"I think you know very well about what. Unless you talk about everyone behind their back." It makes me wonder if they've discussed me. I make a mental note to ask her after we've cleared this up.

"It's just talk. Speculating, or should I say fantasizing, about who might be gay is one of our favorite hobbies."

"This is a person's private life you're discussing." I *am* starting to feel like the principal who has called in a naughty student.

"Just so we're clear." Charlie eyes me with a narrowed gaze. "We are talking about Ida Burton here?"

I nod. "That's who you and Liz were talking about."

"We should have been more discreet." She bunches her fists into her pockets. "I'm sorry."

"It could have been someone else overhearing. It could have been Ida instead of me."

"Oh, shit." She exhales and shakes her head. "It's not an excuse, but you have to admit that that scene we shot today was, hm…" She scratches her tousled hair. "It was something special and ever since Ida and Derek divorced there have been rumors or, well, maybe I should call it wishful thinking."

"I told Ida about what you and Liz were saying, so if she's a bit frosty with you, you'll know why."

"Oh, shit, no. You told Ida?"

"What was I supposed to do?"

"Hm… *not* tell her," Charlie says matter-of-factly.

I guess it was an option. Maybe something other than Ida's best interests got the better of me.

"It was just some talk, Faye. We meant no harm. Nor did we invent this rumor about Ida." Charlie displays her palms. "She's been single for years. There has been no one else since the divorce. Her ex-husband is openly gay. People talk. That's what they do."

"It's not because you don't know about it that there hasn't been someone else since Derek."

"Sure, but that kind of proves my point, because the someone else we never heard about might have been a woman."

"Your imagination's too active."

"That particular affliction happens to pay very well in LA." Charlie stands there grinning for a minute, then her grin disappears. "Do you think I should apologize to Ida?"

"God, no, Charlie. Don't do that. Don't ever mention it to Ida, okay?"

"How did she react when you told her?"

"Don't worry." I purse my lips. "You don't need to get

93

Ava to call her to ask if you'll be fired from your own movie."

"I'm sorry about that, but you weren't very forthcoming with information. I figured you'd be more open with Ava."

"Just… keep gossip to a minimum, please. You know how these things can take on a life of their own if enough people start tattling."

"It's nice that you're looking out for Ida like that."

"She's a nice person and you know it's not a given for either of us to do this movie. We don't need on-set rumors to add to our stress."

"I know. I know." She holds up her hands. "When the A-list takes a risk on behalf of us queers, we should all just be stupidly thankful and shut the fuck up."

"Charlie, that's not what I meant."

"I know and I really appreciate you doing this movie. I really do. I just wish it wasn't such a big deal in this specific way, you know? Because the reason that it is a big deal is the exact same reason why someone like me is still deemed a lesser person by so many people in this town and in the world at large, just because of who I love."

"You're right, but that's what we're trying to change." If this is how Charlie feels, I can only imagine how Ida must feel in this town that doesn't want to accept her for who she is. At least Charlie and Ava walk the red carpet together the way Ida and Derek used to.

"You never answered my question," Charlie says. "How did Ida react?"

"She was upset."

Charlie fills her cheeks with air and slowly puffs it out. "Sadly, that kind of proves my point again. In a perfect world, there would be no reason for anyone to be upset about a rumor like that."

"But this world is far from perfect." I should change the subject before Charlie interrogates me further on Ida's reaction. I don't want to lie to her face. I'm not sure I could. "Speaking of things that would happen in a perfect world... you were a bit harsh with Ava about her acting skills."

"True." Charlie nods. "But if I'm not going to be harsh with her about that, who is?"

I can't really argue with that, neither can I judge Ava's acting qualities because I've never seen them in action.

Charlie leans over the kitchen island she's been hovering around since she arrived. "I know how this is going to sound, Faye, and I really don't mean to be untoward. If anything, I thought it was absolutely great for the movie, but in the kissing scene... Did Ida linger?" She quirks up her eyebrows. "I mean, I'm not the director and I'm all for actors making the material their own, but that was not really how you rehearsed it, was it?"

"Ida was fully in character." That's what she told me and that's what I choose to believe. "Veronica has been wanting to kiss Mindy for a while at that point."

"If you say so." Charlie wrote the screenplay. She ought to know. "She's a cracking actor, if you ask me."

"She is." Our chat changes direction to next week's shoot on location in Miami and, throughout, I can't help but wonder how this will all play out. Which opportunity Ida will use to come out and how everyone who worked with her on this movie will react. And what Charlie will think of me when she finds out I knew Ida was gay when she and I had this very conversation. Something tells me she will understand.

CHAPTER FOURTEEN
IDA

Going on location always incites temptation. Different surroundings awaken something in me that I usually prefer to stay dormant. Some would call it libido. I would call it that too but I'm trying not to go there. It doesn't help that we've relocated to Miami, where the air is so thick and damp, it's impossible to wear clothes that cover too much skin, for me as well as the locals.

This is also where we will shoot the second kissing as well as the bedroom scene. Lots to look forward to. Or dread.

What does make things easier is that Faye knows my secret now. I don't have to omit certain things anymore when I'm with her. I no longer have to pretend, if only for a fraction of my time, but still, it makes a difference.

Production has set Faye and me up on the top floor of a hotel overlooking South Beach. There's a private infinity pool to which only penthouse guests have access. It's all very swanky and sleek and, once again, I find myself wondering if it's all been worth it. It's a question I will never be able to give a satisfactory answer to. Not until I come out.

"Hey, neighbor." Faye walks out of her suite, an oversized sun hat covering her head. "Do you think you'll be able to put up with me?"

"I should manage." I nod at the ocean view. "How does the Atlantic compare to the Pacific?"

"The sea looks about the same but South Beach is decidedly not Malibu." She comes to stand next to me. "Did I just sound like the most terrible snob?"

I shake my head. "I know you're not a snob, Faye."

"I've been called far worse in my day, anyway." She pulls her sundress away from her torso. "This humidity is something else." She nods at the pool. "I might have to go for a dip in there very soon."

"I might very well join you."

"We can order some alcohol-free cocktails."

"Fuck that." I'm already reaching for my phone. "We're in Miami. We need to drink mojitos."

"Really?" Faye cocks her head. "What about your precious complexion?"

"The thing about big budget movies is that they have the best makeup people."

"They flew Janet over," Faye says. "She works wonders with that brush."

"We'll just have one." I check my watch. "It's not even seven and what else are we going to do tonight." I realize I'm making assumptions. "Unless you have a hot Miami date, of course."

Faye's lips curl into a smile. "Looks like I have one with you."

"I didn't mean to make it sound like that."

She grins at me. "I was just joking." She pulls down her shades so I can see her eyes. "Is that okay?"

She's so sweet and she probably doesn't even know it. "Is it okay to needle me about having been in the closet all my life?" I give a slow nod. "Please, be my guest." It's the only way I have to blow off some steam.

"Better call for those mojitos then. I shall return promptly in my bathing suit."

I order us a couple of cocktails and refrain from asking room service to keep them coming, no matter how tempting it is. To be here with Faye feels more like a holiday than a location shoot, which are often more stressful because time is much more limited when you're not filming on a studio set. There's more pressure to shoot in fewer takes. I'd best nail the next kissing scene. Maybe Faye and I should practice—I stop myself before I can take my thought any further. Besides, Faye's going to emerge from her room in a bikini soon. I'd best make myself look presentable.

Because I almost never treat myself to a cocktail, this mojito goes straight to my head. We're sitting in the pool, shaded by a large umbrella.

"I'm so glad I told you," I blurt out. "I've only ever had Derek to talk to and, truth be told, it sometimes stings that he and Ben are so happy—something he always rubs my nose in."

"As opposed to pathetic single me." Faye's eyes are shielded by a pair of sunglasses, but I can tell by the tone of her voice that she's joking. Maybe that's what I like about Faye the most. She doesn't take herself seriously. By quite a few standards, and despite her fame and status in Holly-wood, there are those who would judge her for her lack of husband and family.

"I almost feel sorry for you." I turn my gaze back to the ocean ahead.

"At least you have the excuse of being a closeted lesbian. What excuse do I have?"

"Excuse for what?"

"For being single and having zero children," Faye says.

"Uh, maybe you were a bit busy."

"While I've seen co-stars struggle to balance family life with being away from home so much, it's hardly that big a deterrent. I think it would be unfair to blame the job."

"Maybe not the work, but all that comes with it. Ulti-mately, a lot of men are intimidated by fame," I say.

"Or by having to live life in the spotlight and being followed by a convoy of paparazzi everywhere they go."

"Surely that couldn't have been the issue between you and Brian?" The mojito buzz makes me extra forward.

"It wasn't."

Wordlessly, I look at her. If she wants to tell me what caused the demise of their relationship, she will. If she doesn't, she'll change the subject.

"We wanted to have children, but it didn't happen. Neither one of us dealt with it well."

"Oh, my god. I'm so sorry, Faye."

"The relationship didn't survive." She scoffs. "Brian has three children now." It's the first hint of bitterness I detect in her tone. "I have none." She inhales sharply. "I'm happy for him. Brian really wanted to be a father and I'm glad it happened for him."

"What about you, though?" I resist the urge to put a hand on her arm. We're too naked for that.

"After Brian, my relationships never lasted long enough to have the kids conversation, so…" She looks away briefly. "And the clock was already ticking."

"You didn't freeze your eggs?"

Faye shakes her head. "Maybe I should have, but, um, I've been thinking about adoption a lot lately."

"Really?"

"A lot," she repeats. "I'm technically old enough to be a grandmother, but I would need to be a mother first."

"I'm so sorry you had to go through all of that, Faye."

"Thanks. It's, um, not something I often talk about."

A silence falls. The sun, though still hot, is starting its descent.

"Have you never wanted children?" Faye asks.

"Derek and I did discuss it." I wrinkle up my nose. "Although not to have them 'the natural way'. That would never have worked for us." Due to the cocktail I've almost finished, my subsequent giggle is much too loud. "Ultimately, we didn't want to bring a child into our world of lies. Imagine the subconscious damage that would have inflicted on our poor son or daughter?"

"Do you regret not having any?"

"I don't know." I steady myself in the pool. "Anyone who has a child needs to make damn sure they can give them a good upbringing. Honestly, I've never been so sure I had that in me, what with having a lot of my own issues. Like the small matter of being able to accept myself."

"From what you've told me, it isn't so much a matter of self-acceptance as the world not accepting you."

"Maybe, but what's the difference? If I really embraced

who I am, wouldn't it have naturally followed that I made the world do the same?"

Faye shakes her head. "No, and that's the sad part."

Not even Derek has made me feel this understood. Of course, Derek is not a female bikini-clad movie star I'm sipping mojitos with in the pool. I never dreamed of kissing Derek's full, pillowy lips and staring into his delicious grin afterward—despite being married to him for the better part of a decade.

"For what it's worth, Faye, I think you would make an absolutely amazing mother." I mean every word I say.

"Yeah," she says wistfully. "Maybe one day."

"If it's what you want, it will happen."

"What about what you want?" She's pretty good at deflecting conversation away from herself as well. It takes one to know one and I'm an expert.

I suck on my straw and once satisfied that my cocktail is finished, my buzz renewed and my location-induced friskiness soaring, I say, "What I truly, honestly, really want right about now is to make love to a woman again. It's been fucking forever."

Faye bursts out laughing. "Sorry. I wasn't expecting that level of honesty." She sits up a little straighter, pushing herself halfway out of the pool. "Shall I take my leave? I'm cramping your style, aren't I?"

"No, no, no. I'm sorry. I shouldn't have said that. Being here… I don't know. The air in Miami is like horny soup or something."

Faye laughs deep from her belly. "Promise me we'll do this again tomorrow. You're always great company, Ida, but after one of those mojitos, you're freaking hilarious."

"I'm glad you find my unmet needs funny." I figure I

might as well ask now that I've gone this far. "What's your…" I make a vague gesture with my hand. "Situation?"

"My *situation*?" She takes off her sunglasses and cocks her head. "Whatever do you mean?"

"How long has it been since… you know." I thrust my hips forward.

"It's so obvious why you're the one and only queen of rom-coms." Faye slaps her thigh. "You're a real hoot, Ida Burton."

"It's just funny to you because it's me doing it."

"Maybe." She pushes herself out of the water to sit on the edge of the pool. "But tell me this, how long do you mean exactly by 'fucking forever'?"

"I'm talking years here," I admit.

"Seriously?"

I nod gravely. How pathetic I must sound.

"It's not like I can go on Tinder to get a date."

"Isn't there an app for celebrities?" Faye says. "What's it called again?"

"I have no idea, but even if there was, I wouldn't use it, because I'm hardly looking for a celebrity man to get off with."

"Fair enough." She pins her gaze on me again. "How many years?"

I have to take a minute to think. When did I break Martha's heart again—and mine along with it? "Two years and four months." If it wouldn't leave my hair in such a mess, I'd dip my head under the water for a good long while to hide my embarrassment.

"Damn." Even though Faye has taken off her glasses I don't know if that's a look of pity or just utter disbelief on her face. "In that case, you're right. You need to get laid, sister. What can I do to help?"

"Nothing." Most certainly not let me kiss you again.

"Oh, come on. There are always ways."

"Yeah? Like what?"

"I don't know," she says through a wide grin. "I'm not really in the habit of hiding what I want like you."

"I can't just come to Miami and sleep with someone. Not only because I'm in the closet." I pause to better make my point. "One-night stands aren't really my thing. Never have been."

She nods as though she understands. Maybe she's not much for one-night dalliances either.

"Time for the quid pro quo," I say.

"What quid pro quo? I never agreed to anything of the sort." She wiggles her feet about in the pool, splashing up some water.

"Oh, come on. It can't be more embarrassing than my two years and four months, so you might as well fess up. I've shared so much with you already." I add a wink just so she knows I'm kidding about that and I don't expect her to share any long-kept secrets with me just because I have a tipsy need to overshare.

"Hm." She tilts her head back as she ponders my question, exposing the long, smooth line of her neck.

In the pit of my stomach, something tingly takes root. None of this frivolity tomorrow, I tell myself. This ends tonight. I need to nip this in the bud before that innocent tingle expands into something more.

"About eight months," Faye says.

"Acceptable." I inject a smile into my voice.

"Forgettable more like." Faye picks up her empty glass. "My god, what do they put in these?"

"Must be some secret Miami blend," I say as I rack my brain for any gossip on Faye having a new lover about eight months ago. We're here for a few more days. Maybe I'll find out who it was before we leave, provided I don't have to reciprocate that particular quid pro quo now that I've finally put my affair with Martha behind me.

Our phones start ringing almost simultaneously.

"That's Brandon," Faye says.

"Mine's Mark." He has his own special ringtone.

We drag ourselves out of the pool to answer the call of our assistants inquiring what we want for dinner.

CHAPTER FIFTEEN
FAYE

On the fourth day on location, we're shooting both the other kissing scene and the bedroom scene. I'm not sure who decided that was a good idea, but I, for one, was not consulted on this. Maybe they just want to get the intimate scenes out of the way. Someone must have thought it a good idea to schedule our characters kissing in the middle of our stay in Miami.

Ida and I have certainly worked on our chemistry, although, at Ida's insistence, we've not gone the mojito route again. We've had dinner together by the pool, overlooking the ocean, three nights in a row, just the two of us, although the first evening we spent together is still the most memorable.

Last night, I asked Ida if the real reason she hardly drinks is not preservation of her skin, but that she gets rather rowdy after just one cocktail. She gave me a look that said, if only you knew, although I might have interpreted it wrongly.

On the way to the set, which is on a portion of South

Beach today, I keep glancing at today's call sheet. *Scene 15: Mindy kisses Veronica.* The scene reduced to three words. This time, my character has to kiss Ida's. The kiss is to be intense, longer, more passionate than surprising. And Ida's character is supposed to cup my face and kiss me back. All of this leads to Scene 16 on the call sheet: *Mindy and Veronica sleep together.* Our stand-ins will block out the scene for us and it will be so tightly choreographed it becomes sterile, but still. The emotions need to be telegraphed. The intensity of lust needs to be portrayed. Desire must be captured on camera. Although it will all be pretense, Ida and I will spend time in bed together.

She's in makeup when I arrive. She had an earlier call time, shooting a scene with her character's brother—him of the four wives.

"Ready for some smooching?" Janet asks. Makeup artists are seldom intimidated by fame. I suppose it comes with the territory of applying and removing makeup from our faces. They know what we look like underneath it all—just the same as everyone else.

Ida finds my gaze in the reflection of the mirror. She sends me a wink and it puts me at ease. That's how it is with her now on this set. Easy, but with something else in the air. We share a secret. She's been very open with me and I've reciprocated. Some sort of bond has formed although I will only know after this movie is done shooting what it will really amount to. I've become so chummy with co-stars before that I believed I had gained a friend for life only to find the other party forgot about my existence altogether once we wrapped. I've had the opposite happen as well when I played with Brian in a romantic comedy about two inept police officers. Basically, anything can happen, depending on the chemistry that is developed and then either lingers or fizzles. I'm curious to see what will happen with Ida. If it were solely up to me, I'd choose a close friendship.

"We're doing much more than smooching today." I decide to play along with Janet.

"Hey, I should have mentioned this before." Janet leans toward us and drops into a whisper. "But I think it's so great that you're both doing this movie. Brave, even."

Ida fidgets in her chair and whispers back, "Thanks."

I think of what Charlie told me before we left for Miami. In an ideal world, we wouldn't be called brave for portraying two women falling in love in a movie that's been construed as a big summer blockbuster from the start. But this is no time to launch into a speech. The best Ida and I can do for this movie is make sure that our kiss sizzles on screen. Judging from the previous kissing scene shoot, Ida won't have much of a problem bringing the sizzle. Plus, she's Miami horny, but that's not a joke I can crack right now. Not in front of Janet.

"It's really no big deal," I say, instead. "It's the least we can do, really."

In the mirror, Ida sends me a look I can't decipher. I return her look with what I hope is a reassuring smile.

Janet shifts her attention from Ida to me. As she works to make my face camera-ready, I consider that the biggest difference from the last time Ida and I kissed, is that I didn't know she was into women. I tell myself it doesn't make any difference. It shouldn't. But by the time I take my place, I still haven't fully convinced myself of that.

"Action," Tamara says, her voice much less aggressive than when we start any other take.

This is a scene without any dialogue. Mindy looks Veronica in the eyes. They lock gazes. Something stirs in Mindy. A desire she hasn't previously felt. Not even when Veronica kissed her the first time, because that kiss took her by surprise more than anything. This kiss is instigated by Mindy, who is usually very buttoned-up and proper, and doesn't go around kissing people, let alone her best friend. But something inside of her has been unraveling since that first kiss. The rules she likes to stick to. The sense of control she's addicted to. She's willing to let it all go in that moment. I discussed all of this at length with Tamara the day before. All of this emotion bubbling inside Mindy is supposed to be portrayed in the look I'm giving Veronica/Ida right now. Nobody's yelled 'cut' yet so I guess my facial expression is conveying what it's supposed to. Truth be told, looking at Ida, who is utterly gorgeous under any circumstance, and knowing what I now know about her, which is enough to evoke the confusion I need in my gaze, makes acting out these complex emotions easy.

Mindy closes the distance between them. She inhales deeply. Ida smells of the most delicious perfume. When did she put this on? It's the first time I've smelled this divine scent on her. My nose is supposed to travel upward, not more than an inch away from the smooth skin of her neck. I brush away a strand of her wild curls with my fingertip. This kiss is much more deliberate, with all of Mindy's intention behind it. With all the feelings of friendship she's had for Veronica for years and years plus the added physical attraction she's been experiencing since Veronica planted the very first seed with their earlier kiss, from which Mindy had to flee because it was too much to process at the time.

Our lips are so close together now. My hand is in Ida's

hair. Her scent overwhelms me. Her nearness uncoils something in me. I've never been more Mindy, more in character, than I am right now. I let out the smallest of gasps and push my lips gently to Ida's. When she cups my jaw and pulls me near, and our lips have nowhere else to go but to disappear into this kiss, a small unscripted moan escapes me. But I'm a professional. Oh yes, I am. I let Ida take control of the kiss. Against all rules of movie kisses, I feel the tip of Ida's tongue —because this can't be Veronica, can it?—touch against my lips. I let it happen. Because I'm a pro but also because it feels so damn right. Because I want the take to be good but also because being this close to Ida is intoxicating, moreish and... Done.

As per the script, Ida has pulled back. Slightly aghast, and not fully aware what emotion is displayed on my face exactly, I take a step back. No one has shouted 'cut' so I continue. Ida reaches out her hand and I take it.

"Cut," Tamara yells. "Great stuff, ladies."

I inwardly pray for a first-take print because I'm not sure I can do this again.

I'm not sure why but I have trouble looking at Ida. I scrutinize Tamara's face instead, waiting to exhale until she decides on the take.

Joey gives her a thumbs-up. "I don't see how we can get a better take than that."

"How about the light?" Tamara asks. "Wasn't there a shadow on Mindy's face just before they kissed?"

Joey shakes her head. "No. It was perfect."

"Okay, ladies, that's a wrap. Amazing work." She beams us a big smile. "That's A-list for you."

"Not bad for a morning's work," Ida jokes next to me. I can feel her nervous energy radiating onto me.

"We have to give them their money's worth." I certainly inhabited my character fully. But Ida nearly slipped her tongue into my mouth.

"Trust me, you're worth every million."

Finally, I take a good look at her. The tiny part of her ear that peeks through her mane of wild hair is tinged bright red, but otherwise the makeup does an excellent job of hiding how flushed she is. "Do we need to talk about something?" My voice sounds a touch too scolding, probably because I'm hiding some discomfort of my own.

"We should probably go over the next scene. Should be fun." She waggles her eyebrows.

"Seriously, though." I don't know what to make of this.

She looks at me with a gaze so penetrating it shuts me up, a sensation I haven't experienced since I lived at home with my parents.

A guy I recognize as an exec producer waltzes onto the set. "Bad news. We can't use the hotel today."

While he, Tamara, and Joey talk, I turn to Ida, standing right in front of her so she can't ignore me, no matter what kind of look she sends my way.

"Dinner tonight?" I ask.

"Oh, sorry, I can't. I'm seeing some friends who live here. Rain check?"

Even though her excuse is perfectly valid, her refusal takes me aback. We've had dinner together every evening this week and she never mentioned these mystery friends, although, that too is more than plausible. It's not her excuse that perturbs me, it's that she has one. And that she has planned not to spend time with me tonight of all nights, after the scene we shot today.

Joey finds us and says, "There's going to be a scene

reshuffle. We can't do 16 today because of an issue at the hotel. I promise we will lock it down for tomorrow, even if it means I have to shout at someone for the rest of the day." She smiles tiredly. Shooting on location is exhausting if you're part of the crew.

"No problem," Ida says. "Is there a new call sheet for today?"

"Not yet. I'll get that to you asap," Joey says.

Neither one of us is new to this, and scenes are rescheduled all the time. Part of me is glad I don't have to spend my afternoon pretending to roll around in bed with Ida. I decide not to let any tension I feel ruin my mood or my easy rapport with Ida—although it's hard to forget the touch of her tongue against my lips. It's as though I can still feel it and the spot where her tongue met my lip has become more sensitive somehow.

"These friends you're supposedly seeing," I start when Joey is out of earshot. "Are they a means to quench your special Miami thirst, by any chance? I shoot Ida a faux-lurid smile she can't possibly misinterpret.

"I wish," she says on a sigh. "Because by god, I've been thirsty." With that, she walks off, before I can continue my joking around and tell her that, by the way she kissed me, I had noticed.

CHAPTER SIXTEEN

IDA

When I get back from dinner, it's not that late, and I see shadows dancing on the deck outside my suite. Faye must still be up. Maybe she's indulging in a late-night swim. Or maybe she has guests—or one special guest.

I stand closer to the window and recognize one of the voices immediately. Convinced that nothing romantic's going on, I head out. I find Brandon and Mark in the jacuzzi with a bottle of champagne and Faye with her feet in the pool, chatting to them.

"I hope I'm not intruding," I say.

"Ida." Mark is so tipsy, he can barely pronounce the two syllables my name's made up of.

"I invited these two over for a traditional on-location blowout," Faye says. "That's the third bottle they just finished." She chuckles. "It's been... illuminating, to say the least."

"Okay, guys." I walk up to our assistants. "The boss is back and needs her beauty sleep." I bring a finger to my lips. "You two are being way too noisy."

"No one cares if 's noisy when Ida B'ton and Faye Fleming are staying on the top floor. In fact, 's esspected," Brandon slurs.

"Come on, darling." I pick up a towel and hold it out for him. He starts pushing himself out of the tub. "Wait." I look at Faye in panic. "They are wearing swimsuits, aren't they?"

Faye slaps a hand to her chest. "What do you take me for?"

I smile conspiratorially before returning my attention to the men in our hot tub. "Come on. Chop chop. You know Faye and I have a big scene tomorrow."

"That kiss today," Mark starts, not even pretending he's ready to get out of the jacuzzi. "Was so amazing, Ida. I'm so lucky to be part of your life." He looks at me more adoringly than any other person has in a very long time. I almost feel sorry for him. Then I remember he has a fiancé at home while all I have is an empty bed and make-believe kisses with a highly attractive woman.

Faye gets up and helps me to usher them out. We wrap them in bathrobes and towels and send them on their way to their rooms.

"Good night?" I ask Faye once it's just the two of us again.

"Just blowing off some steam." She points at the empty cocktail glass on the table next to the pool. "I might have indulged a little as well, although nowhere near as much as the two drunk gentlemen we just shoved out the door."

"Those devil mojitos?" I sit in a chair by the glass balustrade. It's so dark, I can barely make out the ocean.

Faye nods. "How was your evening?"

"Pleasant." Throughout dinner, even though I hadn't seen my friends for months, I kept thinking how much more relaxing it is to be around someone who knows who I really am—to be around Faye. I also realized that we should probably have a conversation about that kiss today. It was easy enough to brush her off earlier—it's kind of my specialty—but it was hardly fair.

She has wrapped a towel around her waist and sits in the chair opposite me. In the low light, she looks angelic, her skin pale and her jet-black hair cascading over her shoulders. No wonder my tongue wanted to come out and play during the take today. I hope I reigned it in before she could feel it. I think I did.

I take a deep breath and say, "About today, um…"

"We don't have to do this, Ida." Faye's voice is hardly more than a whisper. "We can just let it be what it was without discussing it." Her heel drums on the deck. Is she nervous? Does she want me to drop it? Because while I hope my tongue's indiscretion might have gone unnoticed, what I can't ignore is how Faye, albeit as Mindy, practically purred with pleasure into my mouth as we kissed.

"We can?" I narrow my eyes and scan her face.

She nods slowly, sucking her bottom lip between her teeth.

"No need to practice tomorrow's bedroom scene either?" I nod at the open French doors to my room. "We have the decor at our disposal."

Faye scoffs and shuffles around in her chair. "I'm not sure what you mean, but I'm not gay, Ida."

"I never said you were." I'm taken aback by the sudden sharpness in her tone. "Are you okay? I didn't mean anything by that. I was just joking."

"You do like to joke. I have noticed."

"That's what you do on set, isn't it? To deflate tension? Take the pressure off?"

"Hm." She gives a terse nod, almost a jerk of the head. What's up with Faye tonight?

"Talk to me," I urge.

She huffs out some air. "I don't know. Something's changed between us, but I don't know what it is."

Surely she knows, because it can only be one thing. Maybe she doesn't *want* to know. "For that reason, I do think we need to talk about that kiss." I try to keep my tone as neutral as possible, even though my heart is hammering away like crazy in my chest.

"I'm sorry. I don't know what came over me." She sits up straighter. "It would be easy enough for me to hide behind the big smoke screen of acting, but I'm not okay with doing that. I—I'm sorry."

"The last thing you need to do is apologize to me." I want to touch her. Comfort her. Tell her it's all good and there's no point in twisting herself into knots about this, but I can't do any of that because of how it could be construed. I also hate that she's the one person I've come out to and now this is something I need to worry about. I should have come out to someone more neutral. Someone far less alluring than Faye Fleming.

"I disagree," Faye says. "I know the lines are blurry when it comes to this. I'm sorry I was snippy just now, but I've been struggling with how much I actually enjoyed that kiss. As myself, not as my character."

Did I hear that right? This does not help in stilling my heart. She enjoyed our pretend kiss? "These things happen in the heat of the moment."

"Yes, but, Ida, you don't understand. How can I have enjoyed the kiss if I'm not gay?"

What am I supposed to say to that? "It happens," is all I can think of.

"I invited the boys over tonight because I didn't want to be alone with my thoughts." She casts me a furtive glance. "And because I didn't want to count the seconds until you returned."

How many strong mojitos has she had? I get a feeling it would offend her if I inquired about that.

"What thoughts did you not want to be alone with?" I need to tread very carefully here. Not for my sake, but for Faye's. I don't want to be accused of something I didn't want to pursue in the first place. I need to protect Faye from herself. And continue to keep a tight lid on my feelings for her.

"When I think of Mindy and Veronica..." She curls her lips into a grin, then takes a quick breath and leans back in her chair. "It's impossible for me not to picture us. You and me. Impossible to divorce myself from the character."

"It's probably just some on-set thing." I have no choice but to make light of this. As well as her, I'm also protecting myself. "It's everything blending together. Me coming out to you. This movie. Playing these characters. Getting to know each other and spending time together. Pretending to kiss." Although it seems there wasn't much pretending from either of us. "That's why so many romances happen on set, only to fizzle out again as soon as shooting ends. There's this magical atmosphere that can exist sometimes. But it's not real. This..." I point at our luxury surroundings, the roar of the ocean in the background. "Is not real life. People get caught up. It happens to everyone. It's like a very intense holiday fling."

"For you, maybe, but I'm straight." There's bite to her tone, as though it's all my fault now.

"Yes, I know, Faye. You're very much one hundred percent heterosexual. I get it." I can be sharp, too.

"Maybe…" She stretches out her legs until her feet touch my ankles. "There's only one way for me to really find out."

"Find out what?" My palms go clammy. Oh, no. This is not how this is going to go. No way in hell.

"How straight I am exactly…"

"And what's that?" Her toe has inched up my calf.

"With your explicit permission only, of course." She leans forward. "I would like to kiss you. For real."

I huff out some air and shake my head. "No, Faye. That's not going to happen." I have no idea where I get the where-withal to resist her because it's the last thing I want to do. But I don't want this either. It's not right. If a woman is going to kiss me, even after all this time of being un-kissed, I want it to be for the sole reason that she can't resist me, that she wants me the same way that I want her—not as some half-assed, late-night experiment. I retract my leg and her foot slides to the floor.

"Seriously?" Her lips are curled into an incredulous smirk. "You don't want to kiss me?"

"No, Faye, I do not."

"Somehow, I find that hard to believe." She would be right about that, but still. I might be frisky and into her and totally up for it, but I still have my principles. Besides, who does she take me for? I'm Ida Burton, for crying out loud.

"Trust me. You're going to thank me for this in the morning." I rise. "Maybe it's time to call it a night."

Something crosses her face. "Did I just make a complete ass out of myself?"

"A bit, but don't worry about it." I offer her my hand. "Come on. I'll walk you to your room."

Even though the door to her room is only a few yards away, she takes my hand. I gently tug her in the direction of her suite.

"Sleep well," I say. "I'll see you tomorrow."

She looks down at our joined hands. "Ida, I'm s—"

"No apologies, okay?" I let go of her hand. "Go. Get some sleep."

"Ida…" She turns around. "I'm not drunk, you know. I swear to you that I'm really quite sober and that I—" She stops again.

Walk away, I tell myself. Walk away right now. But I remain standing, enthralled by whatever Faye is going through.

She slants toward me and puts a gentle hand on my hip. "I felt your tongue," she whispers. "You can stand here and tell me to my face that you don't want to kiss me all you want, but your tongue told a very different story today." All of this whispered less than an inch away from the sensitive skin of my neck.

"I got caught up." My voice snatches in the back of my throat. "Just like you did."

"That's exactly right." Her gaze finds mine again. "Just like I did." She looks at me.

I look at her. Time slows. Her hand creeps up my hip, her fingertips reaching under my blouse, connecting with skin, lighting me up.

"Faye," I say on a sigh. "This is not fair."

"Why not?" She closes the last of the distance between

us. Her lips are so near they've disappeared from my field of vision. "If we both want it."

"Please, stop." I don't sound very convincing.

"Okay." I can feel her lips move against the side of my mouth as she says it. "I'll stop." Her breath is hot on my cheek. "If that's what you want." She kisses me lightly just under my cheekbone. "Good night, Ida." She doesn't move. Everything stills. She's waiting for me to take the next step. I'm waiting for me, too. I don't know what to do. I'm torn between what I want and what's right. Are they really so at odds? She just told me this is what she wants. It's not up to me, certainly not at this point, to read and interpret her mind for her. To make decisions for Faye.

I tilt my head back a fraction so I can look at her face. Then, exactly like in the scene we shot today, I cup her jaw in my palms, and move closer. Our lips meet and as soon as they do, her fingers latch on to my hip more tightly. She groans as she did in the scene. It's a sound so enticing, I lean into her again, and deepen the kiss.

She's the one who opens her lips to me first. She's the one who can't keep her tongue under control this time around. She lets it dance into my mouth, meeting mine, reducing the rest of me to jelly.

Faye curls her arms around my waist and presses her body against mine. The towel she wrapped around her waist earlier falls to the floor. I'm acutely aware that she's only wearing a skimpy bikini. One of her hands crawls up my back, to the hair at the nape of my neck.

"Oh, fuck," Faye whispers, when we break for a moment, before she comes for me again. Her kiss is gentle and deep at the same time, awakening something inside me that I've ignored for far too long.

Her other hand moves to my front, underneath my blouse again, her fingertips sending an electric current through my flesh. Finally, I dare to touch her bare skin. I place my hands on her sides. Even though we're kissing and her tongue is all but shy, I'm too shell-shocked to use my hands. To move them about her body the way she's doing.

When she starts to pull me inside her room, I stop.

"Faye, slow down."

"You don't want to come in?"

"You know I want to, but..." I can't have the same conversation all over again. "I'm not going to." A kiss is one thing. What she's inviting me in for is several bridges too far.

"Okay." She flashes the tip of her tongue along her bottom lip. "But at least kiss me good night." She comes for me again, pulling me near, kissing me until I'm dizzy and I'm not sure how I will physically make it to my own room next door.

"Good night, Faye," I manage to say when I finally drag myself away from her. "Sweet dreams."

CHAPTER SEVENTEEN
FAYE

I can still feel Ida everywhere, even though she barely touched me. I fall back onto the bed and listen for any sound she might make in her suite, but the penthouse's walls are soundproof and I don't hear a thing. I bring my fingers to my lips. To where mere minutes ago Ida's lips were glued to mine. What a kiss. How am I supposed to go to sleep after that? How am I supposed to look my best in the morning for that bedroom scene we're shooting? Janet will have her work cut out because my mind is not geared for sleep in the least. It's too busy figuring out what's going on with me. Something that would have been much easier to figure out if Ida was in the room with me. But I've been insistent enough for one night.

I can still smell her, as though her scent lingers in my room, even though she hasn't even been in here. Something of her presence hangs in the air. Or maybe that's because all the things she radiates so effortlessly always leave a piece of her wherever she goes. What I can't wrap my head around is how a woman like Ida, someone so hot and wonderful and universally adored, has denied herself love for such a long time. Even I can't resist her. I chuckle to myself until my chuckle transforms into a silly schoolgirl giggle. I'm reduced to a hormonal mess. So I do what any teenager would do after they've been blown away by a kiss like that: I reach for my phone and open a text message. My fingers hover over the keypad, but I don't know what to type. There's only so much tapping into my inner teenager I can do, it seems. I'm probably too old to be channeling that period of my life. I toss my phone away and take off my bikini. I take a shower to wash the humid Miami night off me and slip between the sheets trying not to think of Ida.

I knew exactly what she meant by on-set magic between co-stars. That's how I met Brian. It all started innocently enough with some mild flirting, followed by a first kiss that blew my socks off, only to all end in heartache seven years down the line. So much for the easy fleetingness of it.

I toss and turn for a while, my mind overrun with images of Ida's lips. My fingers still tingle from touching her. Until I can't take it anymore and I turn on the TV. I flip through the channels until I land on a rerun of *Underground*, the TV show based on Charlie's books, in which Elisa Fox plays a lesbian super spy. As far as I know, playing gay didn't turn Elisa gay. She and her perfect husband have been together forever, defying all Hollywood relationship laws.

The episode is too complicated to grab my attention. All I see is Elisa Fox being clever and hot and fierce on the screen. In a way, she's the one who paved the way for Ida and I to do this movie. She's the one who took the first risk —and it paid off big time for her.

I huff out some air and reach for a bottle of water on the nightstand. I check my phone but there are no messages from Ida. Maybe I should call Ava. She would understand. I feel like I might burst out of my skin if I don't tell someone. But I can't tell anyone. I still need to protect Ida's secret. And my own. Because why did I kiss her? That's the one and only question keeping me awake. I kissed her and I invited her into my room. To do what exactly? Especially after I kept repeating to her that I am, in fact, very straight. The embarrassment is almost too much to handle.

Not that I suddenly no longer consider myself straight, but stating it the way I did was borderline pathetic, especially because all I wanted to do was kiss her—a woman.

Eventually, I wear myself out getting stuck in endless thought loops about what I am or what I might be, interspersed by images of Ida's million-dollar smile, and her soft voice coaxing me into my room, and the scent of her hair, which seems to be stuck inside my nostrils, and I fall into a fitful half-sleep until my morning wake-up call from Brandon. His hungover voice and exasperated sighs sound like the exact embodiment of how I feel inside: tired, on edge, and a whole lot embarrassed.

Thankfully, because of his epic hangover, Brandon is very quiet, which is not something that happens very often. We go through my morning routine swiftly and silently, my nerves revving up and up, until it's time to go to the set and face Ida.

As soon as I enter my trailer, there's a knock at the door. It's Mark, asking if I have five minutes to spare to go over the scene with Ida. I'm pretty sure that 'going over the scene' is code for 'we need to talk about last night', so I say yes, even though I don't really know what to say about it. The kind of night I had has not left me with some deep and meaningful new insights in the morning—on the contrary.

Mark lets me in and then leaves Ida and me alone. She sits there smiling so radiantly, I don't even know how to respond. Any smile of my own I can muster feels wholly inadequate against the wattage of hers. I wish I could look inside her and find out what her secret is. What it is about Ida Burton that makes her so irresistible? Or maybe it's just me. Maybe I've passed some invisible threshold and I'm now in new territory where Ida is the undisputed queen of my attention.

"Coffee?" she asks.

I decline and sit in the chair that is farthest removed from her. I again feel like that silly teenager I turned into briefly last night. I feel I should say a million things but they all want to come out at once so I end up saying nothing at all, just waiting for her to speak. For all of my brazenness of last night, I feel like a shy little mouse under Ida's gaze this morning.

"So," Ida says. "How are you?"

I let out a nervous chuckle. "Fuck, Ida, I don't know."

"Just remember," she says. "It was just a kiss."

Just a kiss? To her, maybe. "Was it?" I look into her smoldering brown eyes and, as I do, as our gazes connect, it hits me that I'm a little smitten with her. And I'm supposed to be the straight one—as extensively repeated last night.

"Yes, Faye." She stretches her arms over the back of the couch, drawing attention to her cleavage. "What do you think it was?"

"I'm—" I sigh at my own exasperation. "I don't really know. I'm very confused right now."

"I bet." Ida slants her head. "Did you get some sleep?"

I shake my head. "Not really. You?"

She sinks her teeth into her bottom lip briefly, then says,

"Perhaps not as much as I should have. Big scene today. Are you ready?"

"It's not that big." Not as big as the kissing scenes, in my opinion, but maybe I'm a little too heavily focused on all things kissing today.

"It's big for the movie."

"Because the audience will forever remember the image of Ida Burton and Faye Fleming in bed together."

"It'll be etched in their memory, Faye." Ida grins at me. "We owe it to them to make it worth it."

"I'm nothing if not a pro, but... look, Ida. I don't even know if I should be apologizing to you or not."

"I told you, no apologies required." She brings her arms forward and leans her elbows on her knees, shortening the distance between us. "What do you have to say sorry for, anyway?"

"Last night, I said that something had changed between us. That was peanuts compared to how things are now. I don't know how to act. I don't know what to say." I don't know what to feel.

"How about we have dinner tonight?" Ida asks casually, as if dinner still means just dinner—the way it did the first nights of the location shoot.

"Yeah. I'd like that." I hold her gaze and wonder how much she is enjoying this. Or is she going to pieces on the inside as well, but she's just a better actor than I am?

"Okay. We'll talk all of this through tonight." She reaches out her hand. I look at it as though she just sprouted it before I calm myself down enough to take it in mine. "Meanwhile, have you seen the changes to the script Charlie and Liz have made?"

"What?" Brandon gave me today's sides earlier, but he

didn't comment on them. "No, that's the first I've heard of any of that."

"I think there was no problem with the hotel room we're shooting the bedroom scene in at all." Ida arches up her perfectly sculpted eyebrows high onto her forehead. "I think Charlie and Liz had some divine inspiration yesterday and decided they needed some extra time to work on the scene." She hands me a few sheets of paper.

I read the altered scene which is much less fade to black than the original and has Ida and me actually rolling around in bed instead of just having a post-orgasmic conversation under the covers.

"What the hell?" I glance at Ida. "You're not playing a prank on me, are you?"

"Nope."

"You don't have a problem with this?"

"No, but, of course, Faye, I know you are like a million percent straight, so it might be different for you."

Now she's just mocking me. "I need to speak to Charlie. And to Leslie. And potentially fire Brandon for not informing me about this."

"Go easy on your poor PA. After all you plied him with booze all night. Brandon looks like he has a very delicate constitution." She merrily shakes her head. "And I've spoken to Leslie already."

"That may be so, but she's my agent too." What the hell is going on here? Granted, rewrites happen on set all the time, and I don't want to be a diva about this, especially if Ida isn't going to be, but I do feel like I should have been consulted.

"If you don't want to do it, we don't do it," Ida says.

"Like we have all the power." I snicker at our impotence when it comes to things like this.

"Charlie's your friend. Talk to her." Just then, there's a knock at the door.

"Are you okay?" Ida asks me before she answers.

She only invites whoever's there to come in after I've nodded.

"Speak of the devil," Ida says, when Charlie appears in the door of her trailer.

"Please don't hurt me." Charlie protects her head as she comes in. "We only put the final touches to the rewrites an hour ago. I wanted to get your take on it."

"What happened to a rom-com not having any scenes like the one you just wrote?" I ask. "And the 'only a bit of super chaste kissing' you promised me?"

"About that," Charlie says. What is she going to do next? Call Ava on me again? "Liz and I changed our minds after yesterday." Charlie waves her hand between Ida and myself. "Something happened between Mindy and Veronica in that scene we shot yesterday. It sparked the idea to intensify the bedroom scene. I took it to Tamara, and I honestly thought she would never agree, but she did, right off the bat." Charlie holds up her hands. "I have no idea what's going on between the two of you, but whatever it is, it's pure gold for this movie. I could never have dreamed that the chemistry between you two would be so crazily off the charts, but it so is, and I think we'd be nuts not to work with that." Charlie casts me a hopeful glance.

"I'm totally okay with this rewrite," Ida says. "I agree with you, Charlie. There is something unquantifiable between us."

Did Ida really just say that? Is she getting more brazen as the shoot progresses? She still hasn't told me what her grand coming out plan is. Maybe we should talk about *that* tonight.

"Tamara's going to come and talk to you in a bit," Charlie says. "We're shooting Scene 19 first."

"I'll think about it," I say, making sure I sound as non-committal as possible.

"Thanks." Charlie says an elaborate goodbye and leaves.

"I know it's a bit more physical than you expected," Ida says. "But it's nothing compared to what you did in *Under the Wind* with Isaac Moore."

Now that's she's dragging previous movies into it, Ida's arguments sound rehearsed, as though she's trying to make something happen that she wanted all along.

"That was a totally different movie." It didn't elicit many laughs, for starters.

"And Isaac is a man."

"Are you getting some sort of perverse pleasure out of this?" I ask, putting the sheets of paper with the rewritten scene away.

"Of course not. It's totally up to you." Someone knocks again.

"Makeup in five, Ida," Mark shouts.

"You too, Faye," Brandon's voice, much smaller than usual, follows.

"I'll think about it." I head for the door. "I just don't like this feeling of being... almost ambushed into this."

"Take some time. No pressure." Ida beams me a half-wattage smile. It's still plenty to light up something inside of me.

CHAPTER EIGHTEEN
IDA

Faye's a real sport. Not a touch of prima donna about her. She's agreed to the rewritten bedroom scene. While Joey's blocking out the scene on set with our stand-ins, Tamara's going through it with Faye and me in an adjoining room.

In the first section, we're supposed to tumble into bed, Veronica on top of Mindy, look each other in the eyes intensely, and kiss—again. This is just choreography and we don't rehearse the kiss, nor do we really look each other in the eye—at least not very intensely. We practice falling backward onto the bed while Tamara directs us vis-à-vis where the camera will be when we shoot.

After last night, it does feel different to have Faye drag me on top of her. There's only so much you can pretend when you're acting. There's always a real person behind the actions and the lines, even though we're playing a character. It's our bodies touching, it's our gazes meeting, it's our own thoughts running through our heads.

No matter what happened last night—and what didn't

happen after I refused to enter Faye's room—nobody on set will know. Charlie might have noticed something while we shot the kissing scene the day before—it was probably hard not to notice—but that won't happen today.

"Let's move on to the next section," Tamara says.

Veronica is supposed to straddle Mindy and, shot from the back, unbutton my blouse. Later, when we shoot, wardrobe will make sure not an inch of my breasts is visible, while the shot of my back will make it look as though I'm naked, but it's still an interesting motion to go through.

"The things we do for money, eh," I joke, as I look down at Faye, while I undo my blouse, underneath which I'm wearing a tank top for rehearsal. She looks like she could do with a laugh.

Her gaze is fixed to my hips. To the spot where she ran her fingers upward last night. Did she really mean it when she invited me in? Did she really want to move beyond that kiss? I might never know. Maybe even Faye doesn't know.

"Okay," Tamara says. "If you could just hold your positions for another few seconds."

Because Faye hasn't given me a laugh yet, as soon as she glances up at me—the way she's supposed to do in the scene—I pull a face. The ripple of her muscles as she laughs shudders through me. It's so infectious that I burst out laughing as well.

"Glad it's funny." Tamara sounds like a sourpuss principal who's about to tell us off, but of course she doesn't. She's working. She's focused. We should be focused too but it's hard when I have my legs spread across Faye's belly.

In the third and final section of the scene, we're lying down facing each other, our faces so close we can feel each other's breath, and Mindy runs a fingertip over Veronica's cheek.

Faye isn't supposed to touch me yet, but maybe she has different rehearsing methods than I have. More hands-on, like when she invited me to her beach house for kissing practice. When her fingertip skims across my cheek, it startles me into a sharp intake of breath.

This isn't a very difficult scene for us to rehearse. We're just lying in bed, gazing deeply into each other's eyes, while Faye touches me gently. Yet, it's difficult. It's hard to get up afterward and pull myself away from Faye's soft touch, from that look in her eyes that might be trying to tell me something that she can't express in words.

"If you can bring that to the shoot," Tamara says, "this movie will go down in history as so much more than a simple rom-com."

"You brought it," Faye says.

"And you." We've been dancing around everything we should be talking about ever since we sat down to a poolside dinner.

"Not everyone can just do that," she says.

"That's why they pay us the big bucks." I push my plate away, indicating that I'm done. It's a hot night again and I've pulled my hair up so whatever breeze there is can cool my neck.

"It's a funny job, acting, isn't it?"

"It is, but it's also exhilarating and worth every minute you spend waiting for a light to be adjusted and every time someone from wardrobe accidentally pinches your skin."

Faye takes a sip of water and tilts her head back. "God, Ida, I can't tell you how much I enjoy your company."

There we go. At last, an opening. "I think you showed me last night."

"I was quite insistent."

"You were." I wish she was walking her toes up the inside of my leg right now.

"It might confuse me, but I don't regret it." She brings a fingertip to her lip, drawing my full attention to her mouth. "You're one hell of a kisser."

"Pity they don't give out Oscars for that." Tonight, I'm not resisting anything. "If they did, I'm sure you'd have more than me."

"No way."

I need her to come to me again because part of me is still terrified that she might see me as the lesbian that came on too strong. "Last night, before we kissed, you said there was only one way for you to find out how straight you were."

"Good god." She briefly buries her face in her hands. "Exactly how un-woke was it of me to say that?"

"Maybe a few points less than the hundred-percent heterosexual you say you are," I joke.

I like that Faye has not let her stardom go to her head so much that she has lost her sense of humor—I've seen it happen much more than I care for. The ability to have a good dig at yourself seems to plummet exponentially with the amount of money you can ask for being in a movie.

Faye erupts into a chuckle. "If last night's kiss has taught me anything," she says, "apart from what a stellar pair of lips you possess, it's that none of that probably matters all that much." She finds my gaze. "Because that kiss was pretty spectacular."

Heat flashes up my neck to my cheeks. I don't immediately reply.

She shuffles in her seat. A fresh round of tension flares up between us.

"I've pondered what you said about on-set romance and the circumstances creating a particular kind of vibe, and I do agree with all that… I just wonder what you think that means for, um, what might or might not happen between us," Faye says.

"Is that your very convoluted way of asking me whether I think we should kiss again?" I look into her blue eyes. I want to sweep that mane of hair away from her neck, and kiss her where her fingertips meet her skin just under her ear.

She expels some air and returns my gaze. "Yes," she says firmly, leaving no room for misinterpretation.

The tingle that took root beneath my belly days ago expands into a rollicking bubble of desire surging all the way through me. "Then what are you waiting for?"

"I figured we needed to talk more first."

"I'm done *talking* about kissing, Faye."

"Yeah…" She pushes her chair away from the table.

I do the same and meet her halfway. We face each other, like we did in bed on set today, but instead of her finger tracing along my cheek, our hands find each other, our fingers interlacing.

"Does it not bother you that I don't know what this is?" she asks.

"Hell, no." It might have bothered me yesterday, but twenty-four hours have passed since we stood in almost the same position. That we're standing here again tonight tells me all I need to know for now. Faye hasn't hidden herself away. She hasn't shied away from shooting a scene that may have an unexpected impact on her career. She's instigated a conversation and has admitted to wanting to kiss me again very much. Only a fool would ask for more at this point.

"You have your location-shoot-induced friskiness to consider, of course," she says, a half-smile on her face. "I get it."

"Thanks for being so understanding."

"No need to thank me because I get to do this." She leans in and presses her lips to mine.

Instantly, heat rises from deep within me. I let go of her hand so I can cup the back of her head to hold her closer to me. The kiss is only hesitant for a split second before it deepens into something so sultry, I can only want more and more.

Faye brings her hands to my sides, her fingertips slipping underneath my blouse again. Flames burst into desire under my skin, and I know in that moment that tonight we will do so much more than kiss. It's the kind of night for it. Hot and humid and heavy with all the right kind of undertones.

When we break from our kiss, Faye whispers, "I want you," voicing my own sentiments perfectly.

"Are you sure?" I have to ask. Even though she just said it, some of my residual fear needs to be alleviated.

Faye nods gravely.

"Because I want you too, Faye."

We stand so closely together I can see how hard she's swallowing.

"Come." I take her hand in mine and lead her to my suite.

As soon as we're inside, Faye comes for me again. She

curls her arms around my waist and pulls me near. Her nose travels along the slope of my neck, as though she needs to inhale my scent. She stops at my ear and kisses the edge of my cheek, working her way to my mouth. We fall into a deep kiss again, lips opening, tongues meeting.

I groan into Faye's mouth because I can't get enough of her kisses. I bring my hand to her throat, my fingertips stroking her neck. Her grasp around my waist intensifies, as does our kiss.

I've acted in many a love scene, always opposite men, and never has it been erotic in the slightest, no matter how much chemistry my male co-star and I displayed according to the director. It was so different with Faye today. Our chemistry was real, not an ounce of it faked, and when she dragged her fingertip along my cheek for the camera, it felt real as well. Like foreplay for this, even though I had no idea this might happen. Yet here we are.

When we break for air, I take a deep breath to calm my foolish heart. It's slamming against my ribcage with reckless abandon, pumping red-hot blood through my veins at a furious speed.

"You're so fucking hot, Ida," Faye whispers and it nearly makes my knees buckle.

Surely she can tell by the way I'm looking at her, by the hunger in my eyes, how much I want her. I might have admitted to her on our first evening in Miami that what I really wanted was to spend the night with a woman, but Faye is not just any woman. She's not a mere means to end my almost two and a half years of celibacy. She's so much more than that. A row of Oscars on my mantel don't make it so that I can convey all of that with just one look. This is not the time for speaking. This is the time to get that gorgeous flowery dress off her.

"Turn around," I reply.

She spins around in my embrace, and before I lower the zip on her dress, I move her hair away from her neck and kiss her there. The touch of her skin against my lips is electrifying and my hands drift to her zip of their own accord, while my lips keep pressing tender kiss after tender kiss to her neck.

I guide the dress off her shoulders, and it drops to the floor. I look at her backside for a moment. At the delicious curve of her hips. The smoothness of her skin. The supple muscles in her back.

"I've never done this before," she whispers when she turns back around to face me.

I reply by kissing her on the mouth. By wrapping my arms around her and pulling her near. Is she frightened? Or is her desire for this erasing any doubts—at least for now?

"We can stop any time," I say when my lips find her ear.

"Stopping is the last thing I want to do." She puts a tiny patch of distance between us. "But, um, I have no experience with, er, this…"

"And I'm quite rusty," I joke, thinking it's a better strategy than faking a boldness I don't really feel—certainly not enough for the two of us. "Yet I'm sure it's going to be amazing." I pull her close and find her ear again. "And hot and dreamy and satisfying," I whisper, my lips smiling against her neck.

Her hands hover at the hem of my blouse and this time she hoists it up. I stretch my arms over my head and let her take off my top. She comes for my pants next, unhooking the button, and the touch of her fingers against my skin there quickens my pulse even more. Is this really happening? Are Faye and I really doing this? All because of this movie—in a baffling case of life imitating art.

She unzips me, and I step out my pants, and then we face each other wearing only our underwear. Faye's is black with a lacy trim and in the dim light of the room her lingerie looks like it's the same color as her raven hair and it makes the paleness of her skin look even more delectable.

We kiss again, our breasts touching, and that's when I start to lose myself. Because I haven't been touched like this in so long. I haven't been naked with another woman for years. And this is Faye fucking Fleming melting in my arms, purring in my embrace, returning my kisses with heated fervor. Her hands are in my hair, loosening it where it was pulled up. She breaks away from me as it drops to my shoulders.

"God, I love your hair," Faye says. "When the light hits it in a certain way, it's like it's on fire."

My hair may look like it's on fire, but beneath my skin, I *am* on fire. A hot blaze burns a scorching path through me at the sight of Faye. At how she wants me. At how her hands caress their way from my shoulders, down my arms, to the curve of my back, and then lower. She pulls me near, and we kiss again, and I slowly start walking us to the bed.

Once we've had our temporary fill of deep, hot kisses, I throw the covers back and invite her into my bed. We lie down facing each other, again, like on set today, and she strokes my hair while she gazes into my eyes.

"Shall we go to sleep now?" she jokes.

I can't help but smile my widest of smiles.

"Oh, god, Ida," Faye groans. "Your smile."

It seems to only widen even more at her response to it.

"I have something more fun in mind than sleeping." I scoot closer and bring a hand to her back where I unclasp her bra—skillfully with one hand despite being wholly out of practice.

"Impressive." She beams me a gorgeous smile back and then proceeds to do the same to my bra. "The skills we learn for the movies."

Though equally impressed by her dexterity, I'm stilled by her bra slipping down. I reach for it and slowly guide it off her, exposing her breasts to my eager gaze. Once her bra is fully off, there will be no stopping myself. I need her like this humid Miami evening needs a violent thunderstorm. I need to feel her, taste her, have her. I need her to say my name when she comes. I need all of Faye Fleming for myself just for one night.

CHAPTER NINETEEN
FAYE

When did I start to want this? Because as I lie in Ida's bed, it seems like something I've always wanted. It seems so obvious. She's so beautiful, so utterly mesmerizing, and, clearly, so very hot for me. Ida and I are hot for each other. My brain is too suffused with lust to wonder what any of this means. Whether this makes me a lesbian or just gay for Ida Burton. All I know is that I want this. I want her hands on me, her fingers hooking under the cups of my bra and baring my skin so Ida can lay eyes on my breasts. I want to see the look in her eyes when she does. There it is. They widen a little, then darken with desire. Her mouth opens as her fingertip skims along the side of my breast, approaching my nipple oh so slowly.

My nipple hardens for her. She circles it and an arrow of lust burrows its way from deep inside me to the surface of my glowing skin. To where Ida can touch it, can touch me. All I want is to surrender to her. It comes so easily, like the desire has been building inside of me for weeks without me being aware of it. I want Ida Burton. In this moment, it's as simple as that, although part of me already knows it won't stay that way. But we're hidden away in a luxury suite in Miami, making it feel as though what we do here won't have any long-term consequences.

Ida's finger skates along my nipple and the touch, however light, takes my breath away. Not only because she is who she is. When it comes down to it, she's just a woman like me, made out to be much more than she is simply because her face appears on the big screen every so often. But as spectacular as Ida may look, and she does look as enthralling off-screen as on, I've seen her vulnerability. She has confided in me the great price she's had to pay for it all. She has allowed me a glimpse into her soul, a look at her true self, and that's why I'm gasping underneath her touch right now. Because of the two Ida Burtons I've come to know. The unmistakable, unescapable movie star, and the person behind the mask. The woman who loves other women and right now, I'm that other woman.

As Ida kisses a hot path from my lips to my nipple, as her mouth hovers over my breast and my nipple aches for her so much that I can't keep a small gasp from escaping me, I'm aware of at least one thing: this is the real Ida Burton. And the real Ida Burton is very much into me.

Her tongue against my nipple ignites a pulse between my legs so fierce I push them together instinctively. But it's like Ida sees everything and she rolls on top of me, her knee pressing my thighs apart.

Her lips latch on to my nipple as though they never want to let go, her tongue flashing against it, revving up the heat at the apex of my thighs. I bury my hands in her gorgeous hair, her trademark along with that killer smile. As her lips kiss their way to my other nipple, I know that I'm most definitely not just doing this for Ida. I'm doing this for me. Her touch is so soft, so gentle, so caring yet so intentional— the eagerness of her upper thigh between my legs betrays her increasing lust.

She lets go of my nipple and pushes herself up. Her bra still clumsily hangs from her arms. I help her get rid of it and then I feast my gaze on Ida's breasts. Her nipples are small and tight and I find myself reaching for them as though I can't help myself, as though it's all I've ever done in my life. I cup her breast and she lowers it to my mouth and I respond to her invitation by skating my tongue along one hard little pebble of a nipple. The groan that emanates from her throat does a fine job of vocalizing my own pleasure, my own desire for her, which, up to a few days ago, I didn't even know I had in me.

I cup her other breast, rolling her nipple between my fingers, the way I like it done to me, soft and hard at the same time, just to see how she will react. She pushes herself more toward me, her knee touching that delicate spot between my legs, and I suck her nipple deep into my mouth and surrender to Ida a little more.

She pulls away from me and kisses me deeply, her tongue claiming my mouth, claiming me. Then she gazes into my eyes for an instant and she doesn't have to say it because I know what comes next. She kisses me everywhere again, my cheek, my neck, my nipples, then trails a circle around my belly button, making my clit strain against my panties. She scooches down farther and hooks her finger-tips under the waistband of my panties. She locks her gaze on me as she drags them along my legs and tosses them into the room somewhere. Then I'm fully naked in front of Ida Burton and I haven't been this aroused in a very long time. My clit pulses wildly for her. My skin aches for her. My nipples harden further for her.

She looks at me, pausing for an instant. Maybe she wants to make sure I'm still down for this. A doubt I need to erase quickly.

"I want you, Ida," I whisper.

The side of her mouth quirks up and she gives me the smallest of nods, before returning to the spot where she stopped kissing me earlier. Her lips trail along my lower belly, only now, there's no more barrier of fabric between me and her, between me and the lust-filled air around me, and I give myself up to her. Her red mane of hair is fanned out over my belly and slowly, slowly, is dragged downward, as Ida's lips travel lower still, and kiss the inside of my thigh.

I open my legs wider for her so she knows how much I want this, how much I want her. I touch her hair and it's so soft and velvety, it's an erotic sensation to touch it, to run my fingers through it, because it's such a quintessential, iconic part of her.

She has slowed the speed at which she bestows kisses on my skin, taking her time, savoring me, and driving me completely and utterly beside myself.

It seems like hours later when her lips approach my pulsing clit and the tip of her tongue gently touches down.

"Argh," I moan. "Oh, Ida." My fingertips still against her scalp.

And then she licks me. Ida's tongue feasts on me, slips inside me, drinks me in. She sucks my clit into her mouth. Runs her tongue along the length of my sex. Pushes me onto that higher plane of arousal that is so hard to reach on my own, that's only accessible when two people say yes to each other in the way we have tonight. Or maybe Ida's tongue is just exceptionally skilled. My clit is no match for its deftness. I can feel my climax starting already, slowly, as though my body's not used to this kind of pleasure anymore and it needs to reacquaint itself.

Ida shifts a little, breaking the rhythm of her tongue, and the building drumbeat of my burgeoning climax. She looks at me from between the curtain of her wild hair. With her gaze on mine, I feel her fingers trail along the patch of inner thigh her lips kissed earlier. My toes curl with anticipated delight. Her fingertips slide through the wetness that has gathered between my legs and I brace myself for Ida entering me, for that delicious moment when she slips her fingers inside me and my climax will start building again.

My head falls backward when she slides her fingers inside me. I try to look at her but my body goes limp with lust, my muscles are defenseless against the fire consuming me from the inside. Against the storm that Ida's fingers inside of me unleash beneath my skin.

I buck against her, a groan worthy of the wildest animal leaping from my throat. Until my body stills because Ida's tongue is on my clit again, circling it, while her fingers push inside me, and her hair tickles my belly, and I'm lost to her. Lost to her touch. Lost to the tandem of her tongue and fingers claiming the most exquisite climax from my body. It rolls through me with full force, stiffening and relaxing my muscles, making me yelp like the most helpless creature alive.

Fuck. What did she just do to me? For the life of me, I can't remember ever having come like this, with such force and such utter abandon. But of course my brain is not working properly, its function severely impaired by the orgasm that has just torn through me. I'm usually the kind of woman who's up for more than one round of climactic fun, but all energy has been zapped from my limbs, and my blood seems to flow slower through my veins.

Ida slides out of me gently, places one last kiss on my thigh, then comes to lie next to me.

"Fuck," is all I can say for the first few seconds. So instead of talking, I pull her close to me, holding onto her for dear life. "I feel like I should be giving off smoke from the fire you just started," I say, stupidly, when I can speak again.

Ida's hand is warm and soft on my belly, calming and soothing. She chuckles, then presses a kiss to my cheek.

"I'm glad you enjoyed it," she whispers. For someone who was so bold earlier when she looked me straight in the eye, she sounds almost shy now.

"Hey." I position myself so I can look at her face. "I didn't just *enjoy* that."

Then there's that smile. It truly is a smile that can make anything better, but of course I would think that right now, post-orgasm and so foolishly happy.

"My mind was blown, Ida," I say. "And I want more."

"Just let me catch my breath." She ogles my breasts as though what I just said has made her desire for me peak to another great height.

"That's not what I mean." I caress her shoulder with the back of my fingers, then push her down onto the bed. "This is what I mean." I kiss her while slipping my thigh between her legs the way she did to me earlier.

148

"Faye, wait." She breaks away from our kiss. "You don't have to if, um, you're not, you know..."

"Fuck, Ida." I lock my gaze on hers. Her big eyes are a touch watery. Her face is drawn with emotion—or maybe that's just two-and-a-half years of pent-up lust on display. "I really want to. If you want me to."

She nods, her smile half-cocked. "Please," she says.

CHAPTER TWENTY

IDA

Every kiss Faye presses against my skin feels like a flick of her tongue against my clit—even though I don't know what that feels like yet. But the fact that I might very soon find out what it does actually feel like, has my body zinging with lust. I want Faye so much, I can barely stand it. I have suppressed this part of me for so long—maybe too long. Bestowing my attention on her was one thing, but having the tables turned on me, and having her lips approach my taut nipples, already feels like too much.

It isn't just what she's giving me that I'm acutely aware of. It's also what I have denied myself.

Faye's tongue twirls along my nipple and I feel it everywhere. Her thigh is pressed against my clit with only my flimsy panties for protection. And my clit needs protecting from this avalanche of all it's been denied. I should slow this down somehow, give my body time to catch up, but for the life of me, I don't know how. It's not like Faye is going too fast. I'm the one who's rushing ahead, who feels on the brink of explosion already, just at the touch of her tongue against my nipple. She lavishes it with attention, kissing it, and, then, oh my fucking goodness, taking it gently between her teeth and giving it a slight tug.

I swallow hard and try to take a breath, try to calm my heart that's been going at a furious pace ever since we first kissed outside, or maybe since she said yes to wanting to kiss me again while we were still seated, or probably since long before then. My heart's been going a bit crazy for Faye for a while now and, above all else, I must protect my heart. Because the skin Faye has in this game is very different than what I could have riding on this. I could fall for her. It wouldn't be hard. I'm on my way there a little already, if I'm being honest with myself. She's easy to fall for, easy to be around, easy to talk to. And she knows my secret. And fuck, she clenches her teeth around my nipple a bit firmer this time and if she keeps this up, I'll be spent in no time.

She follows up her bite with a tender kiss and that gets me even more. Her soft lips, hot and warm around my nipple.

"Oh, Faye," I sigh.

She looks up at me, letting my nipple fall from her mouth. "You're so fucking gorgeous," she whispers, and I melt a little more.

If she's insecure about any of this, it doesn't show on her face. She pushes herself up to kiss me again, as though what she has said can only be followed up with a deep and passionate kiss.

I throw my arms around her neck and hold her close, my hard nipples pressing into the softness of her breasts. The simple joy of being naked with another woman. Of having her unruly hair splayed across my face, catching in my mouth. Of her smooth skin rubbing against mine. I make a vow to myself here and now to not let myself go without this again. To make some changes in my life that will allow me to indulge in this pleasure time and time again, because life's far too short not to, and I'm not getting any younger.

She kisses her way from my mouth to my ear, and whispers, "Is there anything in particular you would like me to do?" Her lips against my ear stir another round of lust in me. She can do whatever she wants with me, it wouldn't matter. A raging climax is lying in wait, biding its time, exhausting the very last of its patience. She could just look at my clit, just lock her gaze on me, and I'd come. My flesh is on fire for her.

"Just... anything," is all I manage to say.

She smiles down at me. "Okay." Her voice is so gentle, so understanding, as if she knows exactly what I'm going through.

I haven't been a big help so far and perhaps I should be the one guiding Faye through this, but I'm helpless beneath her gaze, her touch. I want her with the ferocity of the long-denied, like a wild animal that hasn't eaten for weeks and has finally found prey to stalk.

"Let's start with this." Faye draws a line with her finger along my lower belly, just above my panties. Then her finger scoots down, and her fingertip drags along my swollen lips, down, and then up again, to end with a circle around my clit. One more of those and I will have flipped right over the edge. I can barely control my gasps of pleasure.

Slowly, with controlled movements, Faye slips my panties down my legs. She trails her finger upward all the way from my calf, over my knee, to my inner thigh. The rush of air on my sex adds to the powder keg between my legs.

I regret not having told her what I wanted, because now that I'm fully naked, now that my desire is given free rein to roam through my flesh, I want nothing more than to feel her tongue on my clit. To feel her warmth envelop the most sensitive part of my body, and to explode into her mouth.

I bring a hand to her hair. "Faye." My voice is so ragged, so breathless, it's barely audible.

She looks at me, her eyes glinting with passion.

"Please, lick me." As I say it, as I give in to my own ultimate desire, I wonder if I'm asking too much of her. As far as I know, this is Faye's first time with a woman, aside from that kiss when she was younger. "If you want to," I quickly add.

She doesn't say anything, just looks at me as her finger scoots closer to my clit. She repeats the earlier pattern she drew over my panties and my hips shoot up to meet her touch.

A small smile plays on her lips. She leans toward me and whispers, "I want to give you everything you want, Ida."

Oh dear. She might as well have wrapped her lips around my clit already.

With that, she maneuvers herself between my legs and I spread wide for her.

"Oh, Jesus Christ," she mutters and I have no time to wonder what it means because the next thing I know, her tongue is all over my clit, and heat rumbles through my flesh, fire courses through my veins, my flesh tingles, and my mind goes blank.

It's more an earthquake than a wave rushing through

me, destroying all the resolve I built up over the years against loving women, against being with them.

No more, I think, as I let it shatter through me, as I ride Faye's touch through climax after climax until my muscles tremble with exhaustion and my body collapses into the mattress one last time. No more denying myself anything at all.

CHAPTER TWENTY-ONE
FAYE

I wake up in Ida's room with her smell all over me. I push my palms against my closed eyes and think about this movie we're shooting and consider that just as for our characters, a new day has come for Ida and me as well.

For Ida because she's pushing for change, for acceptance, and, ultimately, for love. It's a new day for me because this is definitely a new development in my life. One I'm not quite sure how to deal with. It was all well and good, and sexy and alluring, after dark by the pool. But Ida and I have to be on set in a few hours, playing the same characters we played the day before, even though neither one of us can be the same after last night.

I roll onto my side and look at her sleeping. I can barely see her face because it's covered in hair. She has one arm above her head, the other next to her body, as though she's reaching for me. What am I going to say to her when she wakes up? What do I want to say? I have no idea. What I do know is that what I felt last night was real lust. It wasn't some made-up fantasy about sleeping with a woman. I wanted Ida the same way she wanted me. The reason I know this is because at the sight of her naked body, her chest rising and falling slowly with her breath, I feel the same desire as last night, although slightly tempered because of the hours we spent satisfying our needs. At the very least, it's illuminating for me to know I can feel this way about another woman. But is it more than lust? And, if given the chance, would I do it again?

I check the alarm clock next to Ida's bed. I don't know if she has it set or if she's asked for a wake-up call, or—and this is a distinct and slightly frightening possibility—if she has asked Mark to wake her up, but either way, she should get up soon. After the night we've had, I can't just flee to my room while she's still sleeping. I have to say something. But she still seems totally out of it. Her body probably needs the rest.

When she came the first time, and she just kept on coming as I took her into my mouth, I couldn't believe it —as though her body had saved up years' worth of climaxes and they all kept pouring out. The flush on her cheeks afterward was one of the cutest things I've ever witnessed.

I run a finger along her belly, but she doesn't stir. I'm going to have to be firmer in my wake-up call. I know just what to do. I shuffle closer and bend over. I kiss the side of her breast, then move upward to clasp my lips around her nipple. It springs to life in my mouth. I flick my tongue against it until she stirs. I feel her hand in my hair while she stretches her limbs.

"Oh, Christ," she says. "What are you doing to me, Faye?"

I give her nipple one last naughty flick, then look at her. "Waking you up."

"Oh my god." She twirls a strand of my hair around her finger. "Please tell me it's not morning yet."

"I'm afraid it is, gorgeous." I push myself up so I come face-to-face with her. "Sorry."

"Hey." Despite her obvious fatigue, her eyes light up. "How, um, are you feeling?"

"Pretty tired as well." I nuzzle my nose against her neck. "And sore in muscles I didn't even know I had."

She curls her arm around my shoulders and pulls me near. I inhale the scent of her hair.

"No regrets?" she whispers.

"None," I say truthfully. How could I possibly regret a night like that? I wasn't lying when I told Ida she blew my mind. I just don't know where to take it from here.

"Good." She turns to me so our naked bodies are pushed against each other. "After you fell asleep, my mind started whirring and I was so wired, I stayed awake for way too long."

"I figured you would have been spent." I stretch my lips into a smile.

"I was, but you know how it is when your mind starts going around in circles." She only manages a feeble half-smile. She's going to have to do better than that on set later.

"What had you so worried that you couldn't sleep after all those orgasms?" A small rush of pride surges in me because I was the one who gave them to her—to the great Ida Burton.

"I was worried that I… that this wasn't as consensual as I believed it to be. That I had somehow coaxed you into doing things you didn't want to do."

I have to laugh. "I'm sorry, Ida, but surely I was *very* clear about what I wanted."

"You were, but still… I don't mean to presume, but I imagine last night meant something different to you than it did to me."

"Well, sure, because we're not the same person." If I'm being a little facetious it's only because I don't really know how else to be. I don't know what it is she wants to hear exactly and even if I did, I'm pretty sure I wouldn't be able to say it to her.

"You know what I mean… You've never been with a woman before and it might have… not really gone how you thought it would or felt… I don't know. Like something you never want to do again." She swallows hard. "Because of my completely unchecked desire, I might have missed some cues."

"You didn't miss a beat." I put my hand on her side and let it slip down to her buttock. "I wanted you and it was glorious." I press a soft kiss onto the tip of her nose. "Don't worry about that. Okay?"

She nods, her nose touching mine.

"But now, I have to go to my room before my alarm starts blaring and Brandon arrives."

"Of course." She stiffens against me.

"We'll talk more later." I kiss her on the cheek and start rolling away from her, but she pulls me back to her.

"Dinner tonight?" she asks and I don't know if she just means dinner as in sharing a meal or dinner as in what happened last night.

"Yes." Before I roll out of her bed, I look into her eyes, and give her a quick, furtive kiss on the lips.

Even though Ida and I don't have any more physically intimate scenes left to shoot, our characters have a lot of emotions to process together. One of the scenes we're shooting today has Veronica making a big speech and Mindy reacting cold and aloof. On top of that, the set is abuzz with that particular kind of nervous energy that comes with the last day of shooting on location when there's less time for multiple takes and the old adage that time is money is on everyone's mind.

"Did you and Ida go on a bender?" Janet asks me as she applies another layer of foundation. "Her skin is usually such a dream to work with, but it took me forever to hide the dark circles under her eyes today."

I try to stay still in my seat under Janet's scrutinizing gaze. "Something like that."

"At least you're more forthcoming than Ida. She froze me out at the slightest hint of conversation."

"Give her a break, please. She's just tired and hungover." I can't help but defend Ida. I can just imagine her shuffling nervously in this very chair, not knowing what to say.

"Where did you ladies go? And more importantly, why wasn't I invited?"

"Sorry, Janet." I send her an apologetic smile. "We just ended up drinking too much while lounging in the pool. It's so hot and humid in this town. Before you know it, you've imbibed too much." I nod at Brandon who's tapping away on his phone. "Just ask Brandon and Mark."

"They've invited me out on the town with them tonight. We have a big night of clubbing and Cuba libres planned." Janet winks at me.

"Good for you." I feign a yawn, even though I'm plenty

tired. "It'll be an early night for me so I'm well-rested when the shoot resumes in LA."

"As far as I've been told, we're on schedule, so I should literally be out of your hair in a week, Faye." Janet starts fussing with my hair.

I'm not sure whether I'm looking forward to wrapping this movie or not. I'm not even sure if I'm looking forward to going back to LA. Frankly, at the moment, I have no clue what I want, and it's a deeply unsettling and unfamiliar feeling, but at least, if I can bring these feelings to my character, I should be able to give a stellar performance today.

"Ida's been snapping at Mark all morning," Brandon confides in me as we wait in my trailer for me to be called. "She must really be feeling under the weather." He purses his lips in the most judgmental way, as though he wasn't extremely hungover himself the day before.

Poor Mark, I think. But why would Ida treat her assistant like that? Surely Brandon is exaggerating for effect —it's one of his favorite hobbies.

"He was running lines with her earlier and apparently she couldn't remember any of her dialogue, even though she's been perfectly off-book for days."

Maybe instead of falling into bed, we should have rehearsed today's scene. I check my watch. I have about fifteen minutes until my call time. Should I go talk to Ida? Make sure she's ready for the scene?

"I'll talk to her."

"What?" Brandon looks perplexed. "Why?"

"It's, um, my fault she drank too much last night and she didn't get enough sleep. I'll run lines with her."

"Um. Okay. Are you sure?" He cocks his head and looks

at me quizzically, as though I'm not an actor and this is not what I do for a living.

"Of course." Brandon's as observant as he's prone to exaggeration. Nothing passes him by. But surely he can't be on to Ida and me. There's just no way, unless he has a hound-like gift for sniffing out when two women have spent the night together. I leave him to ponder everything in my trailer and head over to Ida's. I ask Mark to give us a minute and he looks relieved to be dismissed from his duties.

"Are you okay?" I ask. "Rumors of you terrorizing your assistant are flying around."

"It's this scene. I thought I had it, but it seems to be slipping from my fingers. I—" She shakes her head, her eyes sad with desperation. "I can't start messing up again now."

"Maybe you should take a break and trust that you've got this."

"I can't do that, because…" Ida looks at me and starts pushing a hand through her hair, then thinks better of it—she's already been through hair and makeup—and then just drops her hand in defeat. "I'm freaking out." She starts pacing. "This scene… it's suddenly become too revealing. When Veronica needs to tell Mindy why she can't be with her in secret, something inside me just blocks and I can't say the words. My brain refuses to remember them. It's like I'm having a blackout."

"Is it because of last night?" I fully sympathize with Ida. Even though our lives are privileged, the pressure when the camera rolls can be immense, especially when you're working through some personal stuff. It doesn't surprise me that it's all coming to a head for Ida now. She's had a massive release of tension in her body. Her brain might have some trouble keeping up.

"No. I mean, yes, it has to be." She huffs out some air. She glances at the clock above the door. "They'll be calling us any time now and all I want to do is fall apart."

I take a step toward her. "I know this is hard right now." I take her hands in mine. "I know you're confused and feeling insecure and maybe even scared of what the future will bring, but I'm here with you. Say the words to *me*." I tap a hand against my chest. "Don't pretend. Don't act. Just say the words. We'll get through the scene together."

CHAPTER TWENTY-TWO
IDA

The overhead lights are too blinding. The microphone too close. There are too many people on this set. Tamara has too much expectation in her glance. Most of all, I can't rely on my brain. I can't go on instinct or switch to auto-pilot. I have to say these lines and I'm not sure I can. It's as though all the years I've lied about who I really am have come back to bite me in the ass in this moment. All the emotions I have denied myself have been compressed into this vast expanse of unease in my chest. I'm somehow certain that when Tamara yells 'Action' my voice will let me down, my throat will close up, and I might as well stop calling myself an actor.

All of this is happening because all I can really see is Faye. How she yielded to my touch. How it felt to be inside her. How the smoothness of her skin restored, or at least started the healing process of this giant, unnecessary wound I've inflicted upon myself.

I'm astounded by my capacity for hypocrisy, for lying, for the emotional fraud I've committed time after time.

A New Day isn't the kind of movie where bad things happen and huge grief needs to be overcome, yet it feels kind of that way to me. But I can't tell anyone. I can discuss my character's hidden intentions with the writers and the director, but I can't tell them why I'm freaking out like this.

"Don't pretend," Faye said. "Don't act." But that's all I've done throughout my life. In fact, at this very moment, my life is more an act than this movie we're shooting. This romantic comedy requires lightness and well-delivered punchlines and for me and Faye to do what we do best, but it's exactly what's doing me in. On paper, a scene like today should be a breeze for me. Yes, it's a big speech and an emotional moment in the movie, but that's exactly what I've always excelled at. It's what the easy laughs and the big hair and the wide smile always end up leading toward. That moment of crisis before the big hurrah. Even the movies with the flimsiest of plots have scenes like this, and I've always been able to bring it. But all of those other times, I hadn't slept with Faye Fleming the night before. I hadn't become who I really am. I hadn't pulled the mask away from my supposedly heterosexual face.

"Ida," Faye says. "You've got this." She must see the panic in my eyes because she takes a step closer, holding up her hand to Tamara. "Remember what I said." She puts her hand against my upper arm and her touch is hot against me, even through the fabric of my blouse. Her fingers singe, taking me out of my skin, and dropping me right into another memory of last night. Faye's head between my legs. Of course it was almost beyond arousing, but more than that, it felt so right, so like coming home from the longest, most arduous journey. And I know that the reason I'm falling apart now is because I've reached the final stage of my long road home. It's why I wanted to do this movie. It's why this scene in particular spoke to me so much and, when I read the manuscript for the first time, I felt like I had no choice but to do this movie. This road I've been on is not endless, even though it has felt like it at times—felt like I would never make it home.

I know very well that Faye is not my home—it's just what she stands for because of what happened last night. Because being with her has made me feel closer to myself than ever before. Has made a few irreparable cracks appear in my once impenetrable armor.

I've never felt more like walking off set than right now. Not even when having to act opposite a co-star so vile and foul-mouthed, who took cracks at me after every take, that all I wanted to do was slap him in the face. Not even when I played a mother so destroyed by grief, I wasn't sure I had that emotion in me and my fear of failing was far greater than anything I had to portray. Not even when I played opposite Serena Bishop and all I wanted to do was kiss her instead of reciting lines to her.

Owning up to the truth about myself is so much harder than anything else I've done. It should be easy. It should be a relief. I should be ecstatic that I've created this opportunity for myself, that we can even make this movie. That Faye is here with me. But I'm none of these things because all those years in the closet have somehow convinced me that things are good behind my facade of perceived straightness. Maybe not ideal. Maybe not perfectly satisfying. But good. Solid. Making me dependable and always easy to work with. A good sport. Up for anything—except *that*.

"Do you need a minute?" Joey has walked up to me.

I know better than to ask for a minute on the last day of

shooting on location. The good, dependable actor that I am would never commit the cardinal sin of wasting the production's money like that. Besides, I don't need a minute. I need hours, days, months. I can have all the time I need after this movie wraps. I can take a minute after this scene. I just need to find the strength inside me to say these words. Now.

"I'll be fine." Faye's hand is still glued to my arm. If Joey notices this, she doesn't let on. I suppose it's not that uncommon for actors to help each other out, but, to me, that hand on my arm means so much more. Because that's the other nagging thought in my brain: how on earth am I going to stop myself from falling for Faye? Already, it seems impossible, despite all the warning signs flashing neon yellow in my head. "Let's do it." I manage to sound much more convincing than I feel.

"Okay." Joey beams me a big smile. Faye gives my arm one last squeeze. You'd think I'm about to appear in front of a jury to prove my innocence—or my heterosexuality—instead of acting a scene in a movie. This is what I do. This is why I get paid obscene amounts of money. To deliver even when I find it impossible.

"Action," Tamara yells.

As always, time slows down. I'm aware of the cameras, of where I need to go after Faye has said her line—of what I need to say. I have the text in me. It's buried underneath all the shame and guilt. But it's there.

"I can't do what you ask of me, Veronica," Faye as Mindy says. "I hope you can understand that."

Don't act. Just be. Just say the words. Let them flow from your mouth as if they're yours. That's Faye's voice in my head. Kind, gorgeous, understanding Faye.

"I can understand," I say, "but I'm not going to hide this

either. I'm sick of hiding. I'm sick of being the forever-single sister. I'm out for a reason." That was the hardest line for me to say. The one my brain wouldn't allow to drift to my tongue and roll from my lips. It must have been my subconscious protesting. I can hardly blame it—it's been through a lot with a master like me. "Out and proud." Oh shit, did my voice just crack a little. "And I don't expect you to be any of that, Mindy. How can I? But I'm not going back into the closet. I've been hiding in there long enough." Veronica swallows hard. She's not supposed to. It's not in the script. But there you go. It will all be captured by the close-up camera mere inches away from my face.

"What are you saying?" Mindy asks.

"I'm saying…" My voice isn't supposed to tremble like that. "That…" I'm not supposed to hesitate like this. No one's yelling 'cut' so I keep going. The lines that have escaped me since this morning are just there, at the ready, raring to be said out loud. "That I want a girlfriend. A partner. Someone who's not ashamed to be seen with me. My brother just married his fourth wife and me… I still look like I have no one, even though I have you." Surely that didn't come out right, but I resist the urge to look around me. To check if I've landed in a parallel universe where this mumbling is considered good acting.

"It's not about how it looks," Mindy says. "It's about how it feels."

Ouch. That line feels more like a dagger puncturing my heart than a piece of dialogue in a breezy rom-com.

"You don't get it." I take a step toward Faye's character. "And I get why you don't, but—"

"You can be so damn condescending and you don't even know it." Mindy's voice breaks. She starts walking away.

"Mindy! Wait," I shout and I don't even have to try for tears, because Mindy is Faye and Faye is walking away and I can't imagine her doing anything other than that in real life as well.

"Cut," Tamara says.

Faye walks back to me. "That was great." Her smile breaks my heart a little bit. "I never had any doubt you could do this, Ida. None."

I nod and pretend to gracefully accept her compliment.

"Okay, that was really great," Tamara says. "Damn, Ida. Way to go on the breaking voice. Can we try one take where you try to amp that up, please? Unless you feel like pulling back first and being a bit icier about it. I'd like to have some options to work with in post-production."

Now that I've done it once, that I've recited the words for the first time, it's not that hard to do it again with varied emotional undertones. With every take, my resolve for two things grows: take an axe to the closet door that's been keeping me trapped inside as soon as possible, and be very careful with my fragile, untrained heart as I emerge.

Even though we've only been in Miami a bit longer than a week, it feels like the last night of a long summer camp instead of a brief location shoot. As I get ready for my last supper with Faye, I feel like I'm saying goodbye to so much more than a city I can return to any time I please.

I'm leaving a part of myself behind here, part of the old me. I wish I could leave all of the old me behind, but I'm not ready for that yet. And first, I will have one last night with Faye.

I keep my eye on the open door to the deck but I see no movement yet. I head out to wait for her. The French doors to Faye's suite are ajar and I hear voices. I lean over the railing, trying not to listen in. The other voice is male and probably her assistant's, but still, it gives me pause. Because wanting to come out is one thing, but finding myself on the losing end of a fling with Faye will be, in its own way, even harder to deal with. And I have to focus on my coming out. I can't have my attention derailed because I'm nursing a location fling hangover. But, by god, do I want to sleep with her again. Do I want to feel her fingers slip inside me. Do I want to come and come like that again.

"Hey." Suddenly, she's there, beside me in all her glory. "Are we dressing up for this? Because I'm not really in the mood." She nods at the pool. "I'm more in the mood for that and a few cocktails."

"Has Brandon left?" Paranoia is still my second nature.

"Yes. Him and Mark and a bunch of the crew are having a big night out." She stretches her lips into a smile. "Please forgive my earlier question." She takes a step closer. "Because I see you've dressed up impressively."

"Oh, this old thing." It's only a linen Armani suit that cost a couple of thousand dollars.

"It looks spectacular on you." She closes the last of the distance between us. "If you're trying to seduce me, it's working."

I do a double take because I hadn't expected Faye to come out all guns blazing like this. But she's irresistible when she's like this—truth be told, ever since this shoot started, she's been pretty much irresistible to me all the time.

"I am." I happily play along, even though I think we

should talk. But maybe we can leave the more difficult conversations until we're back in LA. We're away from home and it's warm and sweltering and Faye seems to be quite into me. "Thank you for your help today."

"Thank you for, um, a most interesting location shoot." She brings her hand to my cheek. "You've shown me a side to myself I didn't even know I had."

"But what happens on location, stays on location," I say stupidly. Argh. I could kick myself.

Faye just chuckles in response. Above all else, she's just such a good sport about anything. Or maybe she's just very good at hiding her true feelings. Although she wasn't hiding anything in bed with me last night. Every single second of that was real, I know that much. "We'll have to see about that." She curls her hand behind my neck and pulls me near. "But damn it, Ida, I want to kiss those delicious lips of yours again now."

She doesn't have to tell me twice, even though she'll be kissing 'Ida Burton', and not so much the real me I've shown her, the woman who's been hiding behind everything she could possibly hide behind. But the two are inextricably linked. What does it even matter now, when my lips hover close to Faye's? When she's about to slip her tongue into my mouth.

When she kisses me, any resolve I talked myself into goes out of the window. It's no match against the force that is Faye Fleming. Against the heat of her lips, the hardness of her nipples as she pushes her body against mine, against her hand clawing at my hair as though she's adamant to take some of it home with her.

"As this is our last night," Faye says, "I was thinking..." She cuts her gaze to the pool. "You, me, in that pool, without any clothes on."

"I like the way you think."

"As gorgeous as this suit looks on you, let's get it off." She starts pushing my jacket down my shoulders.

Because I need a minute, I say, "I'll take this off inside. I'll be right back."

"Need any help?" She locks her gaze on mine and it's shimmering with something I can't decipher. All I know is that Faye is coming on very strong tonight.

"I'm good." I hurry inside and take a breather. It's as though Faye is trying to prove some kind of point—as if she's trying to out-lesbian me in some way. It doesn't feel entirely natural—not like last night, when everything that happened seemed to happen because there was no other logical way for things to go in that moment.

I put on my bikini and drape over a loose sundress. She might be coming on strong but I hardly think she'll be expecting me to jump into the pool with her *sans* clothing straight away.

A splashing sound forces me outside. Faye's bikini is lying on the ground. She's sitting on the steps in the pool, only her head sticking out above the surface.

Oh Jesus. Faye's naked underneath the surface of the water. But I can't just strip for her like this, can I?

"It feels so good in here, Ida," she says. "Come join me."

Then it feels as though I have no choice—and I couldn't keep my swimsuit on any longer even if I wanted to. Faye's seen all of me. Maybe the water has cooled her down somewhat. Maybe she will be ready to take things a bit more slowly. Or maybe she was just rushing into it all because, she too, feels like time is running out.

I hoist my dress over my head. I resist the urge to turn

around as I unhook the clasp of my bikini top. Instead, I face Faye, and try to make it so she can't look away. But her gaze seems glued to me already. I can't help but wonder for a split second if she's into me the same way I'm into her, even though I know it's not possible.

I hurry out of my bikini bottoms and into the pool, feeling very ogled as I lower myself into the water. It's relaxing, freeing even, to be fully naked in the water, to feel it flow naturally against every last inch of my skin.

"Don't you think it's lovely?" Faye asks.

I nod and take the opportunity to study her face. Did she knock back a few mojitos in her room with Brandon before she came outside? I just kissed her and there was no hint of alcohol on her breath.

"And Janet can't scold us tomorrow for getting our hair wet." Faye pushes herself away from the edge and dips her head back. As she does, her chest rises out of the water, but not enough to uncover her nipples. Somehow, it's more enticing than if she had bared them to me.

She comes to stand in front of me, hair dripping. Even though I'm covered by the water, I'm very aware of how naked I am. A drop falls to her shoulder and I can no longer restrain myself. I brush it off her skin and despite the water, touching her while we're both fully naked feels like fire-works are going off underneath my skin.

"Faye." I caress her cheek with the back of my fingers and she leans into it. "I want you, but…"

"No buts tonight." She pushes her naked body against mine, her nipples brushing against mine. "There will be plenty of time for buts later." She gazes deep into my eyes. "I want you too," she says. "Fuck, Ida, I want you."

As soon as our lips touch, her hands are all over me. I

feel myself spreading for her already. God, how I want her inside of me. The night is young, yet it feels like it might be the very last time already and all of it will be erased by the time we land in LA.

"I'm so happy for you that you got what you wanted," Faye whispers in my ear as her fingertips circle my clit. "That you got to make love to a woman again."

"I never expected that woman to be you," I say as I start gasping for air.

"It is me," she says, and with that, pushes her fingers high inside of me.

CHAPTER TWENTY-THREE
FAYE

I wake up next to Ida again, but we're not shooting today. We just have a plane to catch. Just like yesterday morning, she's still fast asleep. I don't expect Brandon or Mark to turn up any time soon, although I don't know Ida's assistant that well.

My hair smells of chlorine and so does my skin from all the time we spent in the water. We barely talked. We barely swam, either.

Ida let on that she was surprised at how enthusiastically I came for her, but how else was I going to experience my last night with her? Reluctantly? I don't think so.

"Hey," Ida's voice croaks beside me. "Is it time to get up?"

"No. We have some time." I turn to her.

"Then come here." She wraps an arm around me and pushes her warm, naked body against mine. "Let's just lie here for a few more hours then."

It feels so good to melt into Ida's warm flesh, to feel her hair tickle the back of my neck. I could lie here with her for a few more hours, but I hear the soft thud of reality knocking, of real life announcing itself and asking where the hell I've been and what the hell I think I'm playing at. All fair questions and surely questions Ida wants to ask me as well.

We lie in silence in each other's embrace for a while. I'm not sure if Ida's sleeping or snoozing or just holding onto me a little while longer. Heavenly though it is to be wrapped up in Ida's arms, as time progresses, and our flight departure nears, more tension creeps into my muscles, and I can't lie still any longer.

"Getting antsy?" she asks and it's such an innocent question, yet it unleashes a wave of guilt inside me.

I smile at her, and she smiles right back and I consider that she should spare me of those classic Ida Burtons smiles in the future because they are quite the addictive sight to behold, especially first thing in the morning after a night of passion. The hearts this woman must have broken. The pain she must have caused—most of all to herself.

I nod and press my nose against her neck one last time. "You are truly a glorious woman, Ida."

"But?" she asks.

"As agreed last night, let's leave the buts until we're in LA."

"Okay, *but...*" She brings a hand to her mouth. "Sorry." She manages a half-hearted chuckle. "Look, Faye, I think I know what this is. I just need a little bit of clarity. We don't need to have a big conversation. I just need confirmation."

"Excellent avoidance of the word *but*," I joke, because I don't want to be the one to say this. Frankly, I'm not even sure I want to say it. Would another few nights with Ida be so bad? I really can't see any reason why they would be, unless being back on the West Coast flips a switch inside me and makes me unable to see her the way I see her now.

She'll still be Ida Burton, my co-star and the woman who has coaxed orgasm after orgasm from my neglected body.

"Does this end as soon as we get back?" Ida asks.

"I don't know." I trace a fingertip along her jawline. "I wish I did, but I really don't know."

"D—do you want to get together in LA?" Her eyebrows almost touch, so quizzical is her look.

"Maybe." I don't have it in me to say no. And we might as well give it a go. What have we got to lose?

"I wasn't expecting that."

"I can't make you any promises and I don't know if what we've had here will be so easily transported back home, *but...*" I skim my finger just underneath those glorious lips of her. "Oh, shoot."

"The penalty is one kiss," Ida says.

"It's never a penalty to kiss you." I'm already leaning in, but she pushes me down.

"One kiss from me, in a place of my choice." If only she weren't such an utter delight to be around. I let her push me down. She looks over my body as though giving serious thought as to where she will kiss me, before she bends over and kisses me just next to my clit.

"Oh, fuck, Ida. That's hardly fair."

"Fuck fair." She comes to lie on top of me. "As long as I have Faye Fleming in my bed, I have no intention of playing fair." She kisses me on the mouth now, her tongue soft against mine, making me melt into the mattress.

"I was going to get up," I say, when we take a break from kissing. This morning, it feels as though Ida wants to squeeze every last ounce out of us being together, before we go back to our regular lives in LA. I can hardly blame her.

"Oh, well." She shrugs, smiles, and starts kissing me again. Her hand roams along the side of my breast.

My clit has been pulsing wildly ever since she planted that kiss right next to it. I forget all about our pending flight. All I can think, while Ida kisses me straight into heaven, is that this could be part of my regular life, if only I let it be.

"Let's say our goodbyes here," Ida says, as we wait for our cars to the airport. I wish Brandon and Mark could share a car and Ida and I could take the other. But I think Ida is still at the stage where she wants to rouse even less suspicion about us than me.

"I'll see you on set?" I ask. Shooting resumes the day after tomorrow in LA.

"Unless you want to, uh…" It's almost unbearable how cute she is when she's trying to find words she doesn't really have. "Get together before."

"I have a thing tonight I can't get out of…" Even though we're still shooting this movie, my mind has been drifting to the one I'm due to start promoting soon, spurred on by a slew of emails from my agent.

"Yeah." She giggles nervously. "I'm seeing Derek, so…"

"Maybe it's a good thing we'll only see each other on set. It gives us some time to reflect on, um, things." *Way to name it, Fleming.*

"You're right. Things really need to be reflected on very much." I'm not sure if Ida's babbling or slightly mocking me.

"Okay." I stand in front of her. "Thank you for everything. I've never had such a great time on location, and it was a real pleasure sharing that rooftop with you."

"And you." She takes my hand. "Thank you." Her voice breaks a little the way it did during the first take of yesterday's emotional scene. Another thing we haven't talked about yet. So much left unsaid. But this is not the end. Who knows, maybe it's the beginning of something. Ida needs to come out of the closet and I... I'm not sure what I need. I'll take a good hard dose of reality to begin with.

Our kiss goodbye is chaste and sweet, like we're just two friends saying farewell.

CHAPTER TWENTY-FOUR
IDA

"No way," Derek says. "You're lying through your insanely white teeth." He brings his face close to mine as though that would make it easier for him to ascertain whether I'm telling nothing but the honest truth.

"And yet…"

"You and Faye Fleming? For real?"

"It really happened. In Miami. I'm not sure anything's left now that we're back. But I guess I'll find out tomorrow."

"Wait, wait, wait. Back up and tell me everything. Every last little sordid detail."

With a grin so wide it makes my cheeks hurt, I tell Derek about the mojitos in the swimming pool, about the on-set kiss followed by a real one, about our two hot Miami nights together. I leave out that I can't stop thinking about her and that I haven't come up with a surefire way to protect my fragile, yearning heart yet. That, when it all comes down to it, my heart is in Faye's hands.

"That's shooting on location for you," Derek says, disappointingly. I know it's true, but that doesn't make it less annoying. Then he fixes his gaze on me. "I figure that she knows about you being a big old closeted lesbian now."

"I told her before we left for Miami."

"Jesus, Ida. You're bombarding me with all this huge news. Why didn't you tell me? This is a big deal."

"I'm telling you now."

"Hey." He cocks his head. "I'm proud of you for this. I know it's hard and you know that I know exactly how hard, but it'll be so worth it in the end."

"I should probably have a conversation with Leslie one of these days. She should know."

"It might not just be yourself you have to think of now, however." The ice cubes in his glass rattle.

"What do you mean?"

"If things get serious with you and Faye…"

I shake my head. "It sounds so ludicrous when you say that. Like it can't possibly be real."

"From what you just told me, it's very real."

"God, I really need to talk to Faye. I need some answers, but I'm not sure she can give them to me. Not yet. How can I expect her to, when it took me so long to even think of coming out myself?" I pause. "Either way, I feel like I'm about to be royally fucked."

"And that already happened to you in Miami." Derek shoots me a wink.

I don't even pretend to laugh at his lame joke. I have too much tension running through me, too much un-targeted energy I don't know what to do with.

I huff out some air. "I'm really nervous about tomorrow. I haven't heard from her since we said goodbye in Miami. I don't know what to think. I can't let any wishful thinking get the better of me but I can't go around as though she's dumped me already, although dumped is too big a word for what was basically just a fling." If it was just a fling, then why does it feel like so much more than that to me? And where do I even get the notion that it might be more? Am I that delusional? Until I see Faye and talk to her, I won't know.

"You'll see her tomorrow." He refills my glass with bourbon even though we both know I won't drink it because I'm shooting tomorrow and I want to look as fresh as I can. "Keep me posted. As your former very dedicated beard, you owe me that much."

I do chuckle now. "Gosh, Derek. When you really think about it, isn't the fact that you and I got married the biggest joke of all? When you really ask yourself the question… it's so ridiculous to use marriage to hide who we are. As though who we are is so wrong, so unfathomable, that we had to go through that whole charade just so no one would know. Preposterous doesn't even begin to describe it."

"I know. Hollywood has taken a lot from us—"

"No, it hasn't. It's given us a lot, while we have allowed it to take our real selves, our true integrity." I expel a sigh. "That's why I wonder how people will react. Surely I can be embraced as gay in the long run, except maybe by the ultra-conservative bigots, but how can people ever accept that I lied for such a long time?"

"That's where the real magic of Hollywood will come into play. You spin them a tale. A sob story always works best." He leans over the table. "It's not as though you were hiding a criminal record or anything like that. People will understand that you chose to be mainstream instead of being part of a minority. They will."

"I regret hiding it for so long. I really do. Not just for

my own sake, but just because it's been such a missed opportunity to represent. To show people that it's perfectly okay to love who you love. Me marrying you is like the worst lie of omission ever and by actively hiding, I was saying that it's not okay to be gay." I only ever considered what I could lose by coming out, never about what I could gain

"You can't change all the things that led up to you making that decision. Hindsight is all well and good, but you had your reasons. So did I." He offers me his upturned palm. "And hey, I would never have been married to Ida Burton if you hadn't decided to stay in the closet. It was a true honor to be your husband."

I put my hand in his. "At least we didn't have to go through all of it on our own. We had each other."

"Think of the gorgeous babies we could have made." Derek squeezes my hand. "What a wasted opportunity."

I burst into a smile. "I have always loved you, my friend. With zero baby-making on the side."

"So have I." He squeezes my hand again. "I know it feels like everything's up in the air right now, but it's going to be all right. You're a decent person, Ida. And truth be told, flash anyone that million-dollar smile of yours, and they'll soon forget you were ever in the closet."

If only it were that simple. But life is not a movie set and movie stars have a real life with a million complications too.

I hardly said anything to Mark in the car on the way to the studio. He tried to start a conversation but I was too nervous to reply, my stomach all tangled up in knots. All I asked him was to set up a meeting with Leslie at her earliest convenience, which will probably be later today.

When I arrive it's the usual fanfare of fawning over me, walking me to my trailer as if I don't remember where it's parked, and asking if I need this or that.

I only have one question: "Is Faye here yet?"

"She's en route," the production assistant says. "She should be here in a few minutes."

I don't know whether to instruct Mark to ask Faye to come and see me as soon as she arrives. It seems too eager and perhaps disrespectful of whatever choice she's made. As time ticks on since our last kiss, however, I can't help but think if Faye were really into me and wanted to keep seeing me now that we're back home, the prospect might have excited her so much that she couldn't stop herself from letting me know. Yet I haven't heard a single word from her.

So I wait in my trailer, pacing, trying to go over today's sides, until I get called to makeup.

When Mark's phone rings, for an instant I think it's mine. I think it's Faye calling me on the way over here to clear the air or, I don't know, tell me she's crazy about me and she's been going nuts not calling me.

"It's Leslie," he says. "She can see you after you wrap for the day."

"That's fine." Another small matter to deal with. Coming out to my agent. Surely Leslie has gay clients, but if she does, they're like me: stealthy and discreet—or not that high in the Hollywood pecking order. "I'll go to her office."

Mark sets up the rendezvous and I glance at him. What's he going to think of me? And shouldn't I tell him first? More than most, he has a right to know. But I'll wait for Leslie's opinion, although I can imagine what she's going to say. 'Are you sure you want to do this, Ida? Nothing will ever be the same again. Instantly, you will change into someone else in the public's eye.' But I owe it to people like Mark as well as to myself to do this, to stop hiding.

Even though the door to my trailer is closed, I can feel a buzz outside. A nervous shuffling about. A shift in energy that's audible through the densest of doors. Faye must have arrived.

"Be still," I want to say to my poor, neglected heart, but I don't want to alarm Mark.

Waiting is even more excruciating now that I know Faye's on the premises. Will she call for me? Ask to talk before we shoot? Will she allude to what happened between us at all? She has to. No matter if it stays in Miami forever and she tells me she never wants to be reminded of it again, I know, deep in my heart, that the time we shared can't be reduced to nothing. It was something. It wasn't just the Miami air making us crazy. Faye looked me in the eye and said she wanted me. She might have only wanted me for the time we were sequestered in our luxury suites, but there must be some aftereffects in her too, some remaining aftershocks from the earthquake in our bodies that night.

"Can you check if Faye has actually arrived?" I glance at Mark.

"Sure, but, Ida… is everything okay?" There's genuine worry in his voice. "You haven't seemed like yourself since I picked you up this morning."

"I'm a forty-nine-year-old woman, Mark," I hear myself say, "Some days are going to be like this."

That shuts him up and he hurries off. I do feel sorry for him. Why did I even say that? Although it is hormones making me behave this way today, just a different kind than I was alluding to.

He takes his time verifying Faye's presence. He's probably not keen to be cooped in a trailer with cranky Ida. I can use the time alone. I take a few deep breaths. Give myself a little pep talk, until a knock comes on the door. Again, my heart slams itself against my ribcage with reckless abandon.

"Faye's here and they want you in makeup," Mark says.

No pre-shoot visit from Faye then. Fine. I straighten my spine and make my way to makeup, where Janet regales me with a few clubbing tales from her last night in Miami. If only I could tell her about my last night in Miami, but Derek's the only person I can confide in. It makes me wonder if Faye has told anyone. I asked her to keep my secret but us spending two nights together makes it so it's no longer just my secret that she's keeping.

And then, another shift in the air. I see Brandon first, as though he and Faye make up a procession of two and he has to smooth the way for her. He flips his long hair behind his shoulder, takes a step to the side, and then there she is. The same Faye Fleming I've been shooting this movie with, yet she's a very different person to me now.

"Hi, Faye," Janet says. "I'll be with you in a sec."

"Hey," I manage, while shooting her only a furtive glance. Janet's waving a brush about my face and I can't really look to my side. I find Faye's gaze in the mirror.

"Hey yourself," she replies. She holds my gaze for the tiniest fraction of a second. For no time at all, really, and as she looks away from me, I know. Some things don't need to be said in words. Body language is enough. And Faye's body language is saying, loud and clear, that I shouldn't get my hopes up about anything at all.

CHAPTER TWENTY-FIVE
FAYE

I can't look Ida in the eye. I want to, so much. I want to disappear into those gorgeous brown eyes of hers, those gifts of nature that match her amber hair so exquisitely, but I can't. It's like she's overwhelming me right now. The memory of her, of us, has certainly been too much for me to handle. Worst of all was that I had no one to talk to about it, because I promised Ida I would keep her secret and how could I possibly do that if I talked about what we did?

Just as I can't meet her gaze in the mirror, I don't know what to say to her. I'm waiting for the confusion inside me to make way for elation, or at the very least a hint of clarification, but it all remains a jumble in my head.

"Oooh," Brandon gasps from his spot by the door.

I glance at him, worried that I might have subconsciously given something away that has revealed a sudden insight. But he's looking away from me, to the approaching footsteps and when I see who it is, my shoulders relax at the sight of my friend.

"Look who's here," Charlie says.

Ava heads straight for me. I get up and give her a fierce hug she can't possibly have been expecting, but I need something—someone—to hold on to.

"It's good to see you," I whisper into Ava's hair.

"I hope you don't mind me crashing your party today," Ava says, then fixes her gaze on Ida. "I'm sorry. I'm having such a fangirl moment. I hate to be *that* person, but here we are…"

"Next you'll want my autograph." Ida has painted on her movie-star smile and she looks nothing short of radiant as she gets up to greet Ava.

"I won't go that far." Ava takes Ida's hands in hers and I'm jealous of their easy, uncomplicated touch. "But I would love to have you over for dinner some time."

Ida nods enthusiastically. I study her smile—it's genuine, not the one she pastes on when she's greeting fans. "Only if you lick a spoon for me in the way that you do."

Charlie pushes a hand through her hair. "That's a brand-new movie born right here, right now." She whistles through her teeth.

"Yeah right." Ava shoots her wife a quick glance but then aims all her attention at Ida again. "Not if you won't let me act in it."

I guess that's still a sore point between them, although Ava's able to joke about it. I hope it will become part of their history together soon instead of a point of contention.

"I can give you some acting lessons when I come to dinner." Ida is such a delight with Ava.

"As your best friend and neighbor, I hope I can count on an invitation as well." I sneak a glance at Ida, who cocks her head at me.

"I really need you back in the chair, Ida," Janet says. "Sorry."

"I'll see you later, Ava." Ida takes her seat again.

I stand around, desperate to talk to Ava, but she's just arrived and hasn't come to talk to me—she can do that any time. She came to meet Ida Burton. Still, when she leaves, I follow, and take her aside outside the makeup trailer to ask if I can talk to her later, when she has a minute.

"What a nice surprise," Janet says when I rejoin them.

"I love *Knives Out*," Ida says, trying to find my gaze in the mirror again.

I try to look at her. I really do. But whatever it is inside me that's stopping me from returning her gaze is powerful and adamant. As though, if I were to look her in the eye, I would be acknowledging something I'm nowhere ready to admit to myself.

Ida and Janet banter and I try to listen, but I'm too absorbed in the drama going on inside my own head and before I know it, Ida's ready and Janet starts on me.

"See you out there, Faye." Ida looks as though she might put a hand on my shoulder for a moment, but she doesn't. She just leaves and I sit there wishing that she had, ever so briefly, touched me.

As soon as I get the chance, I find Ava and take her to my trailer, telling Brandon we are only to be disturbed for real emergencies.

"She's something else," is the first thing Ava says after I sit her down. "What's it like working with Ida Burton? Charlie can't shut up about her."

I wonder what Charlie has told Ava about the rumors she's heard about Ida.

"It's great. Um, Ava… I need to tell you something."

"Sure." She rests her gaze on me, probably looking at me properly for the first time since she arrived. Not many can resist Ida's dazzling presence. "Are you okay?"

"No," I say on a sigh. "I believe I might be losing my mind."

"What? Why?" She sits opposite me and leans her elbows on her knees. "What's going on?"

"You can't tell anyone what I'm about to tell you. Not even Charlie. *Especially* not Charlie." I know I shouldn't be doing this. But I need to sort through my thoughts and feelings with someone and Ava is the best candidate for that job.

"Okay." She sounds trepidatious.

"I shouldn't even be telling you this, but…" I feel I'm about to burst out of my skin. "It's Ida. While we were in Miami, we…" I might as well just come out and say it. "We slept together. Two nights in a row."

Ava's eyes grow to the size of saucers. "You're messing with me. Surely."

"No." There's enough gravity in my voice for her to know for certain I'm telling the absolute truth.

"I don't understand." Her eyes narrow, as though her brain has gone into a higher processing gear. "I mean, I do, but I don't. What am I missing in this picture?"

"This movie… it's intense, and we rehearsed a lot of the kissing and I guess it was more than that. There was a spark and in Miami, things grew from that spark." I'm babbling like a maniac. "You know how it can be on location, away from reality."

"Hold on." She reaches for one of the bottles of water stacked on the counter. "Charlie did tell me that your first kissing scene was something else, but..." Her perfectly sculpted eyebrows knit together. "You're actors. You were acting."

"Well, yes, when the camera was rolling, of course we were acting, but we spent a lot of time together and one thing led to another..."

"You slept together?" I can't really believe it myself so I can hardly blame Ava for the incredulity in her tone.

It would really help if I could just tell her that Ida's gay and that we started bonding more seriously after she told me, but it doesn't feel right for me to just blurt that out to Ava.

"What was it like?" There's something very different in her tone now.

"It was... out of this world."

"That good, uh?"

"She's Ida Burton, you know?" As if that should sum it all up neatly. "I like her a lot and we've really hit it off. We have so much in common, we've had so many similar experiences, and we understand each other when it comes to so many things. But I don't know what to do..." I run a hand through my hair, ruining Janet's styling. She'll just have to do it again. I need all my body parts to express the disarray in my mind. "I'm not... a lesbian. I know it sounds stupid, but I also know I wouldn't be the only woman in the world to be gay for Ida. She's just so mesmerizing. She's been out of the picture for a while, but I still get a little starstruck around her and now I don't know how to behave. I don't know if what I feel is real or not."

"What *do* you feel?" Ava gulps from the bottle of water.

"When I'm with her... well, when we spent time together just the two of us in Miami, I felt like..." I shake my head. "I want more of what we shared then. I want to laugh with her like we did in that pool in Miami. I want her to look at me the way she did, with those big sparkling eyes of hers, as though all she wants to do is rip my clothes off me. I want to get to know her better."

"There's your answer, then."

"No, it's far more complicated than that."

"Tell me this, though... who came on to whom?" Her eyes are mere slits again, as though she's about to slot in the final piece of a difficult puzzle.

"I guess it was all fairly... mutual."

"Fuck." She chews on the inside of her cheek for an instant. "And I'm not allowed to tell Charlie about this? She's going to cream her panties like there's no tomorrow." She chuckles. "Sorry. This movie's a really big thing for Charlie and she adores the pants off you and Ida."

"You won't have to keep it a secret forever. Just for now."

"Really?"

Oh. I've probably said too much. "I don't know. It all depends on how it plays out."

"Do you know how Ida feels about you?"

I can't be certain, yet I'm pretty sure I do know. "I think she might feel the same way as me." Except for the small detail that Ida's actually a lesbian.

"What are you going to do? Have you talked about this with her?" She puts the empty water bottle on the table. "I didn't get a whiff of any of this when you were in makeup earlier, nor any of the times I saw you two on set together today."

"I know. I don't know how to behave around her. We

haven't talked since we got back. We've put it off and… I've been scared, because I'm afraid to make a wrong move."

"From what you've just told me, you want to be with her and she wants to be with you. So what's the problem?"

Fair enough question. "The problem is I don't want to lead her on."

"Look, you can only feel what you feel and be honest about it. If you do that, how's that leading Ida on?"

I expel a deep sigh. "There's more to the story, but I can't tell you because it's not my story to tell."

Ava studies my face, then gives me a short nod. "I hope you'll tell me when you're ready to share."

I gauge Ava's face. I trust her and Ava knows what it's like to defy the public's hetcronormative expectations of yourself, and even though I very much wish I could explain myself better, I can't bring myself to spill Ida's secret. Ida's about to bust out of the closet and I'm not sure that's something I want to be caught up in, like a piece of collateral damage. "Being back in LA has also been a bit of a reality check."

A knock comes on the door. "Faye? It's not really an emergency," Brandon says through the door, "but you need to get your ass to wardrobe within the next minute."

"Back to the grind," I say.

"I get a feeling this conversation's far from over." Ava rises. "But it's not really me you should be talking to right now, Faye. Talk to Ida. Tell her how you feel. What's the worst that can happen?"

Tabloid headlines for a long time to come. Paps following my every move. My next movie overshadowed by my torrid, scandalous affair with newly out-of-the-closet Ida Burton. My family and friends scratching their head from now into eternity. Forcing myself into being someone I'm not—or not yet. Letting down Ida in the long run because I can't be who she wants me to be. And worst of all: using Ida as an experiment to find out what it is I really want. I can't share any of this with Ava right now, but at least I got to tell her about Ida and me and that's something.

"I'll talk to her. I promise."

"Before you come to dinner at mine." She grins and walks over to me, putting her hands on my upper arms.

Brandon knocks again.

"Duty calls." I give Ava a quick hug.

"Break a leg," she says.

As long as I don't break anyone's heart, I think.

CHAPTER TWENTY-SIX
IDA

As I head out of my trailer to find my car—on the way to having a once-in-a-lifetime conversation with my agent—Faye walks up to me.

"Do you have a minute?" For the first time today when the camera's not on us, she meets my gaze.

"I'm meeting Leslie. Sorry." As much as I want to talk to Faye, I need to get this conversation with Leslie over and done with.

"Oh." I guess we both know that Leslie would wait for me in her office as long as it takes. "Sure." Faye regards me a little more intently. "*Oh*," she says again, as though she has suddenly realized why I'm going to see our agent. "Just a super quick word in private." She practically pushes me back into my trailer, leaving Mark with the same quizzical expression on his face he's had all day. He knows something's up. He's next on my list, but I can't tell him that yet.

"Are you going to tell Leslie about…" Faye starts.

"Not about us, if that's what you're so worried about."

"I—I'm not. I know you wouldn't do that without asking

me first." Faye's right. "Can we talk later? With Ava's impromptu visit, we haven't really had a chance today. Can I come by your house after your meeting with Leslie?"

This is a different vibe from what I've been getting from her all day. She had me convinced it was all over before it had even begun, which I could fully understand.

"Yes." I want to talk to her too. "But I have no idea which state I will be in."

"Leslie's been your agent for so long. Don't you think she might suspect?"

"If she does, she's never let on."

"Because why would she?"

That's the thing with Faye. I don't have to explain things to her. She just understands. I'm of half a mind to cancel my meeting with Leslie and take Faye back to my house, but I fear that if I don't tell Leslie now, while some of me is still aglow with the afterburn of what Faye and I shared in Miami, I may lose my nerve altogether—especially if Faye tells me it was all a big mistake later, which is still highly likely.

"Good luck, Ida. I'll be thinking of you." Will she? "I'll be there when you get back."

Talk about mixed messages. "Thanks." With that, I'm out of there, and on my way to come out to my agent.

Thank goodness for Faye, I think, and the practice I've had with telling her. Still, I'm grateful it's late enough for Leslie's office building to be almost empty.

"How can I help my favorite actor?" Leslie likes to lay it on thick—it's not one of the reasons she's my agent, because

I can easily do without all the faux-flattery. "How's the shoot?"

"I have something to tell you."

"Okay." She walks to the liquor cabinet—it's only now I understand why she would have direct access to booze in her office. "Will I need a stiff drink with what you're about to tell me?"

"Yes."

"You?" Leslie's ability to keep her face expressionless like a mask of steel under any circumstance is one of the reasons she *is* my agent.

I nod. I don't care that I'm shooting tomorrow. Janet has proven very adept at hiding dark circles under my eyes and I have full faith she can do it again.

Leslie pours us each a scotch then sits opposite me in the designer leather couch by the window overlooking Wilshire Boulevard.

I take a sip, inhale deeply, and just blurt it out. "I'm gay, Leslie."

I thought she'd finished swallowing, but she erupts into a coughing fit. "Sorry," she says, after she gets her bearings. "I never thought you'd just come out with it like that—no pun intended."

"What do you mean?"

"I mean..." She leans over and puts a hand on my knee in that tactile LA way. "I'm so glad you've finally told me, Ida."

"You... knew?"

"What kind of agent would I be if I didn't?"

"Uh..." I don't know what to say to that.

"It's a weight off my shoulders more than anything." Leslie keeps surprising me.

"I thought you'd be upset."

"Oh, Ida…" She gives my knee another squeeze, then removes her hand. "I'm not upset at all. I'm just sincerely happy that you've finally told me." She beams me the most genuine smile. "This isn't the nineties anymore. Or the noughties, for that matter. Or the previous decade even. We can work with this, especially with this movie… You have no idea how I was hoping for something like this."

She's right. I'm stumped. I was under the impression Leslie might even drop me as a client, although she never ditched Derek after he came out and he started making her far less money—another reason why I've been with her for so long.

"How did you know?"

"When your husband divorces you because he's gay, a few alarm bells tend to go off in your agent's brain…" She shakes her head. "Over the years, I've had my hands quite full keeping stories about your sexual preferences out of the tabloids, but it's all part of the job."

"Oh my god. Are you serious? I always thought I was so discreet."

"You were. You are, Ida, but some rumors are so persistent, it takes a deft hand to squash them, which I happen to have."

"Thank you, Leslie. I can't believe you never asked me."

"It wasn't up to me to ask you that question. After Derek came out, I figured you'd come to me if you wanted to."

"Here I am," I say, meaning it in more ways than one.

"How do you feel?" She picks up her glass and holds it up to me.

I clink my scotch to hers. "Surprised and… strangely elated, I guess."

A short silence falls. I've known Leslie for so long that it doesn't become awkward, not even after what I've just told her. She's probably processing. Putting together plans in her head on how she can spin this to our advantage.

"Was it this movie?" she asks, after a while.

I nod. *And the woman starring in it with me*, but I can't say that. "I'll be fifty next year and that closet has been stuffy and dark and depressing for way too long. This movie seemed like a good opportunity to force myself to push away the last hurdle."

"Are you… seeing anyone?" Leslie asks.

"As if you wouldn't know if I was."

"I don't always know, Ida. I don't have those special powers of observation."

"No, I'm not seeing anyone." Maybe, now that I've finally started telling the truth about myself, I should try being even more honest. "I mean, there is someone but it'll probably turn into nothing."

She nods as though I've just disclosed the most boring piece of business information for her to digest. "Is she discreet?"

"She…" God, how good it feels to just be able refer to someone I've slept with as a 'she'. "Never mind." Faye's her client too. "As I said, it's nothing."

"It's enough of something for you to mention it to me and for your cheeks to flush when you do."

"I shouldn't have said anything. I'm sorry. I take it back. Can we talk about more practical matters, please?" I resist the urge to flip my hair forward and hide my pinked-up cheeks.

"At the risk of sounding like the cynical Hollywood agent that I am." Leslie flashes me a sly grin. "This might be just what your career needs."

"That does sound very cynical."

"What I mean is that your career doesn't have to go in the same direction that Derek's went after he came out."

"Let's be honest, compared to someone like Faye Fleming"—I hope my cheeks don't start burning again—"my career has been in free fall for a while."

"You just had a quieter few years. There's nothing wrong with that." She taps a fingertip against her chin. "Do you want to make a big deal out of this or just be casual about it?"

"I don't want too much fuss. And I need to tell some other people before we make this public."

"Of course."

"I just wanted to tell you now because, quite frankly, I couldn't hold it in anymore. I just…" Is that a tear pearling in the corner of my eye? I quickly push it away before it can roll down my cheek.

"We're on your timeline here, Ida. There's no rush. You're in charge. I'm just here to guide you and help you and…listen to you, if that's what you want."

"Faye knows," I blurt out. "She and Derek are the only ones who know. And you."

"Faye?" Leslie's eyebrows shoot all the way up.

"I had to tell her. She confronted me with some rumors she'd heard on set and at first I tried denying it, but I just couldn't do it anymore. I could no longer deny this massive part of me that I've forced myself to ignore for so long." More wetness in my eyes. But these are just tears of relief. Of years of pent-up frustration. So I let them streak my cheeks and drip down my chin.

"Do you need me to talk to Faye?" Leslie's tone is suddenly very earnest.

I can't help but chuckle. "No, I think I've got it." Leslie might have been expecting this from me, but if she ever finds out about Faye and me, I suspect her reaction to that news might be a touch more hostile.

"I'm here for you. Whatever you need." She hands me a tissue.

"Thanks, Les." I dry my tears, because I need to brace myself for the other important conversation I'm having tonight. One that might very well make me feel the opposite of relieved and elated.

CHAPTER TWENTY-SEVEN
FAYE

I barge into Ida's house like a whirlwind because I don't know what to do with myself. "Before we talk about anything else, I need to tell you that—" It's only when I really look at Ida that I see she's been crying. "Oh, god. I'm so sorry. I was having a diva moment." I don't know whether to walk over to her and give her a hug or keep my distance—maybe play it safe for now and stay away. "How did it go with Leslie?"

"Turns out she knew all along." There's only a hint of Ida's famous smile on display tonight. "She was just waiting for me to tell her."

"That's good news, isn't it?"

"Yeah, it's just… look, Faye, I know we need to talk about 'us', whatever that may be, but I need a friend tonight more than anything."

"I'm here for you, Ida." Friend sounds good. I think we've done a good job of becoming friends over the past few months. It's what happened when we went beyond friendship that has me all tangled up in knots.

"I'm glad I told her and it's the first step to... I can't say something new, because I've always been gay. But now I know that Leslie knew all along, I wonder why the hell I've been hiding all these years. Because it's also a matter of self-respect, more than anything, really. Where was my self-respect every time I pretended to be straight? Why did it have to take a back seat to so many meaningless things. I just..." She crashes into the couch. "I feel like I've wasted a big part of my life."

I hadn't really prepared to face these existential questions tonight, but I have to be a good friend. I have my own similar questions to answer, albeit on a smaller scale, and my heart fills with empathy for Ida.

I sit next to her, keeping a respectable distance, even though all I want to do is throw an arm around her shoulders and tell her everything will be all right.

"It's not been a waste, Ida. You did things your way, the only way you knew how." I glance at the picture of her and Derek on their wedding day and it's an oversized cruel reminder of what Ida has put herself through. "You're decompressing after telling Leslie, just because things *will* be different now. It must be frightening as well as exciting."

"She asked me if I was with someone." Ida pushes her hair away and seems to regain her composure a little, only now it's time for me to feel a stab of panic course through me.

"Oh."

"I told her that there was someone, but it would probably amount to nothing..."

So much for only needing a friend and not wanting to have 'that' conversation.

"Look, Ida, I—"

"It's okay." Ida extends her arm and presents her hand. "You don't have to say anything. I've been thinking that all of this is hardly fair on you. You just wanted some fun. I just wanted some… well, you-know-what."

I gaze at her hand as though I have the most difficult decision to make. Does putting mine in hers suggest too much? Seeing as words escape me, a physical gesture is all I have. I touch my hand to hers, rub my thumb across her palm. "I feel so ambivalent about all of this."

She nods as though she has no choice but to understand. "We're in such different places. I know that." She lets her head fall onto the back of the couch. "God, I'm exhausted."

I scoot a little closer and put our hands in my lap. I think of what I confided in Ava earlier, about what I wanted from Ida. As we sit here, I still feel like this could go either way and the fact that I do, that I don't have a clear view on this, automatically makes it impossible. Because I'm not sure, and Ida's in no state to deal with my doubts about myself right now.

"What I'm going to say might make me sound like an utter lunatic," I say.

From the corner of my eye, I see Ida rotate her head so she can look at me as I speak. I keep looking straight ahead.

"I like you, Ida. I think you know that. I like being around you and I think it was pretty evident I enjoyed our, um, time in bed together. A lot." She gives my fingers a quick squeeze. "But we're not on a level playing field here because if we were to pursue this, then I'm not sure if I could ever fall in love with you and that's not something I want to do to you. You don't need that sort of wishy-washiness in your life right now. You're ready to come out. You deserve for this moment to be totally glorious, and you deserve to be with someone who knows with absolute certainty that she'll fall for you, that it's inevitable because she won't be able to stop herself no matter what." I pause to take a breath. "I can't be that person right now, but that's no reflection on you. I need you to know that."

"That's what I figured when I saw you on set today." Ida sounds resigned rather than hurt.

"It's not that I don't want to try… dating you, but… I feel like that wouldn't be very respectful toward you." I finally look at her. "I don't know if I'm making myself very clear. To be honest, it's not very clear to me either."

"I understand you don't want to be caught up in the whirlwind I'm about to unleash on my life."

"It's not so much that." Although, yes, of course it is also about that, but I don't want to rain on Ida's personal pride parade even more.

"It's okay." She gives my hand one last squeeze, then retracts hers. "I get it. I really do."

"I don't want to hurt you." Why does this feel like it's hurting *me*? "I so want for you to be happy."

"I want the same for you." She huffs out some air. "I'm sorry, but today's been a bit much and we have an early call time tomorrow."

I wouldn't want me hanging around any longer either after what I've just said. "I'm sorry."

"It's ridiculous to apologize for something you don't feel," Ida says matter-of-factly.

It's not that I don't feel it, I want to scream. It's not that I don't want to kiss you all over again, have your hands roam all over my body again. Wake up next to you again.

"You're going to make a very lucky woman so happy one day." Christ. If any more platitudes make it out of my mouth, I might start barfing all over myself. And I already despise myself a little for being such a coward about this. But for all the reasons I just gave Ida, I have no choice.

Ida just gives me a curt nod and escorts me to the door.

"Hug?" I ask sheepishly—and utterly stupidly.

"I'd rather not, Faye. I'll see you tomorrow."

My heart breaks a little as I get into my car. I wonder if it's because now it feels like we're not even friends anymore and Ida needed a friend tonight? Or is it because as soon as she said she needed a friend I knew I couldn't be that to her —because I want more? It doesn't matter. I've made my decision. Instead of asking the driver to stop at my house, I ask him to drop me off at Ava's next door.

It's late and Ida was right, our call time tomorrow is earlier than usual, but I won't be able to sleep, and Ava's the only one I can talk to.

I can see the lights on in the house behind the fence, but it takes forever for someone to reply to my insistent ringing of the intercom.

"Faye?" Charlie asks.

"Sorry for stopping by so late. I should have called."

"It's okay. Come in."

By the time the gate has opened and the car has dropped me off, the front door is ajar. I walk inside to find Charlie obviously hastily dressed. Ava, who didn't bother with pretending she was dressed in the first place, is just wearing a robe.

"What's wrong?" Charlie ushers me in. "Is it tomorrow's scene?"

"No. God, Charlie. I'm sorry. You were clearly, um, otherwise engaged. I'll just leave. I—I came to see Ava."

"Don't be silly." Whereas Charlie makes me feel more than welcome, it takes Ava a little while to warm to my late-night presence.

"Can you give us a minute, please, babe?" Ava pulls Charlie near and makes no bones about kissing her deeply in front of me. "I'll be up to finish what we started soon." She sends her off with a fat wink and a slap on the backside.

"I'm mortified." I hide my face behind my hands and peek at Ava through splayed fingers.

"Don't worry about it." Ava pulls her robe a little tighter around her. "I take it you spoke to Ida and you need to process."

I drop my hands and nod. "I told her I couldn't do it."

"Do what?" Ava gets up and, without asking, pours us each a glass of white wine.

"Get involved with her."

"Why not?" She pushes the glass in my direction.

"Because she's going through this massive thing." I have no choice but to break Ida's trust. I need to tell Ava. "Ida has just come out to her agent. It's only a matter of time before it's all over the news. I… I couldn't see myself playing a part in all of that."

Ava's eyes go wide. "Say that again, please?"

"Ida's gay." I huff out some air, because I'm disappointed in myself for not keeping Ida's secret. "She told me a few weeks ago."

"After which you promptly jumped into bed with her?" Ava takes a large sip of wine.

"What? No. That's not how it was."

"Damn it, Faye. Please don't ask me to keep this bombshell from Charlie as well."

I don't know what to say to that, so I heave another deep sigh.

"You do have feelings for Ida?" Ava asks after a few moments have passed.

"Yes, I do, but..." I look into Ava's face. She seems to have absorbed the shock of me outing Ida quite well. "What was it like for you when you met Charlie? You'd never been in anything serious with a woman before her."

"And now we're married." She smiles as she says it. "Charlie and I getting together was a complicated affair." She giggles. "And it was confusing and infuriating and frustrating at times, and I didn't really know what I was doing, but in the end, it didn't really matter because I was crazy about her."

"Weren't you afraid you might end up hurting her?"

"No more than she was afraid of hurting me."

"I told Ida she should be with someone who can be certain about wanting to be with her."

"As if you're not."

"No. I'm not. And it's the doubts that are killing me."

"Even the most successful relationships start with the same doubts you're having now, because there are never any guarantees. You may think you can never feel the same way about Ida as she feels about you, but the truth is you don't know that. No offense, but it might actually be the other way around. It's not because Ida's a lesbian that's she's going to love you more or forever. All of that's just bullshit—well, fear, actually."

I take a sip of the wine. "Of course, I'm afraid. I can't just launch myself into an affair with Ida Burton. It's so far removed from any expectations I have for my life."

"Sometimes you just have to take a leap and not care about the outcome." She closes her eyes, a smile appearing on her lips. "If you had told me five years ago I would come out by bidding on Charlie at a charity auction, I would have told you that didn't fit into my life expectations either." Her smile grows wide.

"That was pretty crazy."

"My point is that when someone's worth it, *you know*. You feel it. You can't shake it. It's inevitable."

I've pretty much been single since Brian left me. No wonder I'm so afraid.

"How do you know?" My voice is so small and tight, I drink more wine hoping I will find some of my mojo.

"I can't tell you that, Faye. You're the one who needs to know."

I twirl the stem of my glass between my fingers and am reminded of what those fingers have done—where they've been. Inside Ida, giving her pleasure. It's hard to believe that my fingers are even capable of that, as I sit here feeling mightily sorry for myself.

"Look… you're still shooting a movie together," Ava says. "You have time to figure this out. There's no need to force anything. But when you see her tomorrow, that first glimpse you get of Ida on set, try to really check in with how that makes you feel. If you feel relief because it's all over, then that's that. Then you know. If you feel something else. Something much stronger. Then you'll also know."

"But that's the thing… All I feel is confusion. Conflict. Ambivalence."

"Welcome to the human race." Ava grins at me.

"But you just said that when I know, I'll know…" Maybe I should have called before barging in and disturbing Ava and Charlie's lovemaking. Her head's all fuzzy and she's not making all that much sense anymore.

"Trust me. You'll know. Some people just need more time than others. There's no shame in that." She gazes at me over the rim of her glass. "Just don't string her along, and always be honest, with yourself and with her. That's all it comes down to. Although"—she grins—"I'm making it sound very simple right now, and it was nowhere near as simple as that for Charlie and me in the beginning. Sometimes it can also be maddening and complicated and slow, but that's also okay." She puts her glass down. "Just don't deny yourself something potentially wonderful because you're scared. That would be a royal waste." She beams me a smile. "*Capisce?*"

I return her smile. "Thank you." I nod. "I'll let you get back to whatever it was you were doing." I waggle my eyebrows at her and make my way home.

CHAPTER TWENTY-EIGHT
IDA

On set the next day, I hide behind an oversized pair of sunglasses, as though they can make me invisible. Even though I only told Leslie, it's like I've come out to the whole wide world already and I don't know how to wear this newly out identity. I'm not used to it. It doesn't feel like me yet, which is a damn shame, because it is me, the one I've been hiding all these years.

It's easy enough to ignore Faye; it just takes a bit more diva-like behavior. But I have Mark as a last line of defense and Mark never lets me down. When I tell him to keep Faye away from me, and make it so we're not in makeup and wardrobe at the same time, that's exactly what he will do. I wish he'd do it with zero questions asked, but that's not really his style.

"You and Faye were so chummy. You were living it up by the pool in Miami every night. Why the sudden frostiness?" he asks.

"You know I adore you, Mark," I say, "but that's frankly none of your business." Wait times seem much longer now that Faye and I are keeping our distance, and I can't afford to alienate my closest ally. Besides, it's about time he knows —if, like Leslie, he doesn't already.

"Let's have lunch together," I say, "unless you have other plans."

"Of course I don't have other plans other than having lunch with you."

"Put your phone away for a minute. I need to tell you something."

"Sure."

As I prepare the words, I realize I can't wait to do this over and over again. To tell the world. To tell every last person on this earth. Because to announce myself this way feels so freeing, so life-affirming, so exhilarating, it almost makes me forget about the—let's face it—very flimsy affair Faye and I had.

I'll get over Faye Fleming soon enough. She was right when she said I deserve to be with someone who will adore the pants off me. I've waited long enough. I can't settle for anything less. Once I'm out, I'm not going back into the closet for her. Not that I think it's only a matter of bad timing. Faye's not a lesbian. It's as simple as that. I knew that from the get-go, even though she was all in when she was in bed with me. That much I also know.

"Please forgive me for not telling you this a long time ago, but I'm a lesbian. If anyone deserves to know the truth about me, it's you."

Mark's mouth falls open. "You're fucking with me."

So that's the reaction of someone who has no clue. Is it because he's a man and they notice different things than women?

"I'm not. I'm gay, Mark. As gay as they come. Hell, as gay as you."

"That's *very* gay." He giggles like a schoolboy in the face of his first crush. "So very fucking gay." His giggles are infectious. I'm getting giddy as well. "You've been gay all this time that I've worked with you?"

"All my life." I explain my fake marriage to Derek and why I've stayed in the closet all this time.

"Wow," is all he says for a good long while. "Is that why you and Faye fell out? Because you told her?"

"No, and we didn't fall out. She does know, but that's not why..." I don't know how to talk about Faye with him. Because of my need for privacy, I've never discussed details from my personal life with Mark—there was never much to share. "I need you to not tell anyone about this just yet. Leslie and I are thinking about the best way for me to go public."

Mark rises and opens his arms wide. "Can I give you a hug?"

"Yes, please." I can sure do with one. My bed's never felt emptier than now. That's another reason I want to come out to the world as quickly as possible. So I can finally meet someone and not have them sign a dozen nondisclosure agreements before anything happens. So I can fall in love with someone like a normal person and not like someone with a secret in her heart and a massive chip on her shoulder. So I can start putting Faye behind me.

I hug Mark and it feels good to have someone wrap their arms around me. It reminds me of when Derek and I hugged. It made me feel safe and loved in a non-romantic way and always just a little bit better about myself.

A knock on the door breaks up our hug. Mark checks

who's there. I can tell it's Brandon but they're whispering together, and I can't really make out what they're saying.

Mark turns to me. "Faye is *begging* for one minute of your time," he says.

We're in a movie together so I can't ignore her all the way. "Fine."

"Do you want me to stay?" Mark gives me a worried look, as though I've suddenly become a lot more vulnerable. Maybe that's how he felt when he started his coming out process.

"No, thanks."

Then it's just Faye and me in my trailer. She's looking gorgeous again, like she's glowing with good health and all the good fortune she's had in her life—although from what she's confided in me, I know it hasn't all been good. That's not how life is. But you can never tell that from looking at Faye Fleming. I guess that's why people are so drawn to her.

"I know I'm your least favorite person right now," she says, "and I fully understand, but you should know that I, um, told Ava about our time together in Miami. And I also told her about you, um, being gay. I'm so sorry, Ida, because I know that was not something for me to share with anyone else, but I had to tell someone. I had to share with a friend. I was going nuts keeping it all inside. I thought you should hear that from me."

Maybe I should be angry, but that kind of fear-based anger already seems to belong to a previous version of myself. "It's okay." This cat's not going back into the bag. "I'm starting to tell more people. About me, I mean. Not about us." A smile breaks on my face. "I just came out to Mark."

"You did?" The smile on Faye's lips can't possibly be fake. "That's wonderful. I'm so happy for you."

"He's asking questions about us, though... about why I'm so frosty with you."

"So is Brandon."

"The set's probably abuzz with it. You know how it is."

Faye's smile fades. "Are you okay? The way we left things last night was a bit—"

"You don't have to worry about that." I'm surprised by the sharpness in my voice. "In fact, I would appreciate some space."

"Sure, but we are still doing this movie together. We have a week of shooting left."

I know I'm hardly being fair—none of this is Faye's fault. "You're right, but... it's hard to pretend nothing happened. For me to pretend with you, I mean, not with everyone else." I'm very experienced at that. I scratch my chin. "If that makes sense."

Her blue eyes rest on me, her gaze soft. Finally, she nods. "Of course, I'll give you space. Anything you need."

"Thank you."

She lingers idly by the door as if she wants to say something, but then she opens it and disappears—again.

———

"Here's to your new life." Derek raises his glass. Again, I find myself breaking my own rule of not drinking alcohol while shooting a movie. It's gotten worse as this shoot has progressed. My liver will be happy when we wrap next week and my body will be hoping for not too many reshoots. "I'm the only one who can say this to you, but it's about time, Ida."

"You won't hear me say this twice, but you're absolutely right."

"I've always understood why you decided to stay in the closet." Derek takes a sip from his drink. "Especially after what happened to me when I came out."

"You've always been so much braver than me." My turn to raise my glass. "We should be drinking to you every day of the week."

"We can debate the merits of coming out versus staying in the closet in this wretched town until the end of time," Derek says in his calm voice. "Sadly, both have merit. Straight actors get Oscars for playing LGBT characters, the other way around…" He gives a mirthful chuckle. "Not so much."

"It's because of what we represent." I shake my head. "This dream. This elusive fantasy."

"Whereas we're all just as mundane as everyone else, we just live in fancier houses."

"Nah, I've always thought you were endlessly more fabulous than anyone else I've ever met."

"Must be why you married me." Derek shoots me a wink. "But seriously, Ida, you coming out is going to be a big deal because it's one of the many steps Hollywood needs to get over itself. To prove that openly gay actors can deliver at the box office."

"Because that's what it's all about in the end: money, money, money." I might be money-rich, I've often thought, but I'm not life-rich. The public may fantasize about me all they want, that doesn't make me loved in real life. That's the big irony of the preposterous double standards Hollywood actors are meant to live by.

"I'm really curious what this movie's going to do," Derek says.

"Movies with gay characters are all the rage right now."

"That may be so, but not big-budget rom-coms starring Faye Fleming and Ida Burton falling for each other...with one of the main actors freshly out of the closet."

"Some of the studio people may have a heart attack." I should really come out sooner rather than later, so that the studio has time to adapt and get their ducks in a row for when we start promotion. "But there's no clause in my contract prohibiting me from coming out, so..." I should actually check with Leslie about that, but surely she would never let me sign anything of the sort.

"Even though I was relegated from the A-list to the B-list and can barely still consider myself C-list these days, I've never regretted my decision," Derek says. He's been part of an ensemble cast in a TV cop show for the past few years, earning him a more than decent income, but nowhere near the millions I can still command, even after having been in a few movies that were less than impressive at the box office.

"I'm sure some TV exec will have room for me on one of their shows." It's easy enough to joke about. "Anyway, TV's where it's at these days."

"Maybe some streaming service can create a show just for us. Something about beards and self-acceptance and all of that," Derek jokes. "As long as we can keep on acting."

I nod because he's right. Of course, it's much easier to get offered a meaty, challenging part if you're ultra-bank-able, like I used to be and Faye is at the height of, but there are plenty of parts out there, waiting to be played the hell out of by the likes of Derek and me, and the gazillion other actors who no longer wish to portray heteronormativity. It won't be as glamorous, perhaps, but we'll always get by. I, for one, don't really have that much left to lose.

"Because fame is overrated, anyway."

Derek rolls his eyes as if he's the one who's just said it and wants to emphasize the point. A short silence falls between us, then he asks, "How are you going to do it? How are you going to bust out of that closet?"

An idea's been brewing in the back of my mind, but I'm not entirely sure yet. I'll have to wait and see how I feel in the moment. "Still thinking about it, but expect an increase in phone calls from the press about your ex-wife between now and, let's say, two weeks."

CHAPTER TWENTY-NINE
FAYE

I've been waiting for that moment Ava has described to me. The moment I know. The moment I feel secure enough to take that leap. Even though Ida's pretty much been giving me the cold shoulder all week, I'm getting closer. Because we did still have all our scenes together to get through and even though it's pretty obvious she's trying to avoid being in the makeup chair next to me, sometimes there's just no other way. Then I try to catch her glance in the mirror, although she rarely lets me hang on to it for more than a split second. But I can still look at her and have an ocean of memories wash over me. I can admire her from afar for who she is and how she carries herself and the decisions she has made about her life.

I'm in the car on my way to the studio for our very last day of shooting, when my phone rings. It's Leslie.

"How's my favorite actor?" Since Ida and I got so well acquainted, I know she uses this opening line with at least two of her clients, but most likely all of them.

"I'm fine." First, we discuss the promotion schedule for a

movie I'm in that will come out in a few weeks, until Leslie goes uncharacteristically silent.

"Ida told me you know about, um, her," Leslie says. I hope she'll be more eloquent when discussing it with anyone else.

I know all about Ida and so much more. "She told me she's gay and she finally wants to come out of the closet."

"What was your first, honest reaction?" Leslie asks. "Remember, this is me you're talking to. You don't need to sugarcoat anything."

I can't give her my most instinctual reaction, because then I would have to admit that I wanted to kiss all of Ida's insecurities away and tell her that I thought she was even more fabulous than before she told me. "Good for Ida," is what I say. "Good for everyone, but most of all, just good for her, because I can't believe how long she's been hiding and how much of a burden that must have been to her all these years."

"You didn't think, there goes our movie?" Leslie is equal parts smooth- and straight-talker.

"No, of course not."

"As in you will stand up for her when you're doing promotion when the movie comes out or as in you'll stand by good-naturedly, but silently?"

"Why would I be silent?"

"I'm behind this coming out one hundred percent, but I have business to think about. I have to manage mine and Ida's relationship with the studios and production companies. I need to know if we have allies and, well, you're the only one who knows so far."

"Half the crew of this movie is gay," I state the obvious.

"That might be so, but it's not the same as one of the leads being openly gay."

"I will stand by and defend Ida as much as she needs me to."

"You might want to brace yourself for some rumors about yourself after this movie comes out."

"Oh, please." If I cared about rumors about myself, I wouldn't have been in this business for this long. "I don't care about any of that."

"That's good to hear, Faye. I'm glad."

Why does this still have to be such an issue, I want to scream at my agent. But we both know why. Movies sell fantasies. Fantasies make money. Money is everything in this town. And change is achingly slow.

When Ida makes her entrance at the wrap party, I wonder if she's had Janet redo her hair and makeup, that's how glamorous she looks. Or maybe it's the unburdening she's been doing of late. It's the relief of no longer carrying around her secret that has had an immediate effect on the smoothness of her skin and the bounciness of her hair. If she's suffering from me no longer wanting to be with her, it doesn't show. Ignoring me between takes all of this week must have really helped her. And she has prospects now. And some upcoming free time to explore her options. Although she hasn't officially come out yet.

Everyone in the room seems to gravitate toward her, like she's a force of nature, or she has a magnet for a heart, and we're iron filings. Because it happens to me too. I find myself drawn in her direction, wanting to be near her, wanting to catch a snippet of what she has to say—just like that first time we sat down together for the table read of this movie.

"Hey, Faye." Tamara has walked up to me. "I can't thank you enough for your work on this movie. I have a feeling it's going to be something special. You and Ida really had this thing going and it comes across so clearly on the screen."

I bet it does. "Thank you for saying that and thank *you* for making this movie." From the corner of my eye, I can see that the crowd around Ida is thickening. I try to refocus on Tamara, who has been amazing throughout the entire process. I don't tell her that even though I think *A New Day* is a wonderful movie, with an important point to make, I suspect it won't get taken all that seriously because it's a comedy and it won't win any big awards for the same reason. There's no Oscar category for on-screen chemistry.

"I'd like to say a few words, please." Ida raises her voice.

Are we starting on the speeches already? That's quick. I haven't really prepared anything, but I'm curious about what Ida has to say.

Despite the elated post-shoot party vibe, the room goes quiet immediately. All this time in the closet may not have brought Ida much love, but it has earned her the ability to silence a room and have all gazes trained on her when she wants them. I'm no different. When Ida Burton speaks, we all listen.

"Okay. Let's do this." She flashes us the brightest of red-lipped smiles. The kind I can feel all the way in my belly—and beyond. No matter what Ida says, the crowd's eating out of her hand already. Or is it just me?

"I want to tell you something," Ida continues. "I want to tell you what making this movie has meant to me." She finds

Tamara, who's still standing next to me, in the crowd. Or is she looking at me? Either way, my palms go damp. Because, suddenly, I have an inkling of what she might want to share with us.

Oh, Ida. If I'm correct, I couldn't admire her more than in this very moment.

"Thank you to everyone who has made this movie possible. All the audience ever gets to see is a finished product of two hours, but we all know the blood, sweat and tears it takes to make a movie. It's a hell of a long road from when the writers have the first idea to when the public gets to sit with a bag of popcorn in their hands and enjoy the fruits of all that labor."

If Ida's acting career were to take a nosedive, she can always go into politics. Or public speaking. She's a natural. The way the light catches in her hair alone is enough to give her a halo of supreme attraction. That aura around her that draws you near and makes you want to never leave her side. Or is that just me again?

She calls out a lot of people by name, impressing me with yet another skill. Truth be told, some of them, like the executive producer she mentions, I've never even heard of. I guess she's been paying better attention. Or she had Mark do some research before she prepared this speech. Because she must have prepared. She's an expert at making it look casual and off-the-cuff, but it can't be. Not if I'm right.

"I'll let you all get back to the booze soon." She injects her signature bubble of light-hearted laughter. "But first…" She's been talking for five minutes now and you can still hear a pin drop. "I need to thank my co-star, the ever-fabulous Faye Fleming."

Her gaze cuts to me. I look straight into her eyes and then, as goose bumps break out all over my skin, I do know.

I know that I've been a fool to risk squandering what we could have because, yes, Ida is being all Ida Burton up there, with all her easy charm and grace, but I've seen the real Ida. I know what she's like behind that mask she's been wearing. I know she's kind and funny and caring and sometimes deeply sad and very frustrated about certain things. I've bowed my head between her legs and felt something so strong surge inside me, I've been afraid to recall it, for fear it might actually mean something. But it does mean something.

It means everything.

"Faye gave me…" She pauses and my pulse quickens. My breath hitches in my throat. "Much more than any other co-star ever has and she's every inch the professional you'd think her to be and more." She looks over in my direction. Her lips curve a fraction into an almost-smile. If only she could tell all these people the truth. I wouldn't care one bit. I would feel only pride standing next to her like that, for what I really mean to her—or I should say *meant* to her. "Thank you so much, Faye."

I give her a nod and a smile back, because, for now, it's all I can give her. And I take her *thank you* for what it is: Ida's way of telling me we're good. Only, now, I'm sure that's not enough for me anymore.

I smile at the round of applause I receive from my fellow cast and crew. I have no idea how I'm going to follow up Ida's speech, probably with a few hastily mumbled words of my own.

"Also…" Ida's voice sounds even more commanding than when she started. She seems to have grown a few inches taller. Her shoulders look squarer. "I want to share with you why making this movie has changed my life."

My pulse speeds up again. *Go, Ida.* I wish she could feel how I'm rooting for her.

"Because..." She swallows something out of her throat. "I'm a lesbian."

A collective gasp echoes through the small crowd.

"I'm gay, guys, and I've felt the need to hide that forever, but no more." Her gaze drifts to me. "No more."

I beam her my widest smile.

"Doing this movie has given me the courage to finally come out and I can't thank you enough for that. All of you. Every single one of you who has made it possible. Every single one of you who has been out for ages, even if it was hard, even if you had to pay a price. You're all my heroes, just for being you. Because, for the longest time, I haven't had the courage to be me. Until now."

Oh fuck. I'm not going to be able to keep my tears from flowing. I'm so proud of Ida. All I want to do is hug her. All I want to do is kiss her.

CHAPTER THIRTY
IDA

Faye's smile is what does me in. Not because I can't be with her, but because it's so gorgeous, so heartfelt, so straight from her to me. It's as though everyone else at this party ceases to exist, even though I just came out to all of them, not caring that some of them have their phones out, their cameras pointed at me, because they want to capture the moment Ida Burton said, in public, for the very first time in her life, that she's a lesbian.

All I see is Faye. Despite making the decision to come out before we started shooting, before we worked together and grew closer—before our passionate time together in Miami—telling her first has made it infinitely easier, has paved the way for this moment. Her confronting me with what she heard Charlie and Liz say about me that day accelerated my process, made it real, so that I could have this moment today.

"Thank you," is all I have left in me, because my throat is swelling with emotion, even though I had a closing joke prepared about being on the market—to speed up the process of getting over Faye. Of leaving all of that behind me and finding someone who can love me the way I love them.

Faye slips out of focus as everyone erupts in applause and whoops and fist bumps. A tidal wave of warmth gushes over me at the support I receive. This is the right crowd for it, of course. And yes, damn it, I did it. I came out.

When I try to find Faye's face again, she's no longer in the spot I saw her in last. Where is she? Did I make her uncomfortable when I stared into her eyes like that? In front of me, the crowd is parting. There's Faye. Walking toward me. How utterly lovely that she wants to be the first to congratulate me—even though she was already the first.

She comes to stand next to me. The crowd's still rowdy with the energy of my revelation. It's probably on social media already. I should have given Leslie a heads-up, but I didn't want to jinx it. I didn't know I was going to do this until the very last minute. Until I did it.

"Please," Faye says, "I would like to say something as well."

It takes a while before the roar dies down. Faye shuffles nervously beside me. Then she turns to me, looks me in the eye, and takes my hands in hers.

"Whoop!" someone yells from the back, and is immediately shushed, but I tune it all out easily, because why is Faye looking at me like this? Why is she standing here, with her hands wrapped around mine?

"Ida," she says, on a barely audible whisper. She drops my hands, brings hers to the back of my neck and, in a rather familiar motion, draws me near.

My heart hammers away in my chest. No way. What's happening? Did my heart just give out? Did I die and go to heaven? Is Faye really pulling me in for a kiss in front of the entire cast and crew?

Her lips touch against mine, tentative at first, but not for long. Her hands roam into my hair and draw me nearer. She opens her lips a fraction, allowing our tongues to touch briefly. Anything more would be obscene, is all I can think. Because my brain doesn't know what's happening. My body's going into overdrive. Can I throw my arms around her neck as well? How will she react? What is she trying to say exactly? As far as displays of support go, this one's very elaborate.

Fuck it. I curl my arms around her and we kiss and kiss and the world around us dissolves into nothing, because this is all I've wanted since we've come back, since that last time I kissed her in my room in Miami.

We kiss until we have to break apart. The noise filters back in and it's deafening all of a sudden. What has Faye done? She must have seen those people with their phones out. *This* will be all over social media now.

"What are you doing?" I whisper, as soon as I get the chance.

"What I should have done last week," she says. "I've missed you."

"Is this for real?"

She nods, shoots me a wink, then turns to the crowd. "Just in case anyone got any ideas in their head, Ida's mine," she says.

"That's a bit possessive," I whisper in her ear.

"Sometimes you just have to make a stand." She's smiling from ear to ear, possibly completely unaware of the repercussions of what she has just done.

"You're crazy." I can't let go of her. If it were up to me, I'd never let go of her again. "Leslie's going to have a stroke."

"What's the point of you coming out if you can't be with me?" Faye asks.

"I didn't come out to be with anyone specif—" I start saying, but Faye kisses me again, so I can't continue.

"On second thought, don't answer that," she says.

"Are you ready to face the music?" I acknowledge the mob of people going mental around us.

"I can do anything with Ida Burton by my side." Faye interlaces her fingers with mine. "As long as you take me home after."

In the car on the way to my house, my lips still zinging with the aftertaste of Faye's kisses, I look her in the eye again. "Are you sure you're not going to regret this?"

"No." She gazes at her phone, which she switched off long ago, for fear it might spontaneously combust with all the messages arriving. "I'm not sure of anything. This is me taking a leap." She flashes me a smile. "This is me living in the moment."

I scoot a little closer, even though I'm almost sitting in her lap. "You didn't plan any of this?"

Faye shakes her head. "No, but you looked so irresistible and inspiring when you were speaking. I had to do something." She puts a hand on her belly. "Because I knew. When I was watching you come into your own like that, I knew…"

"What did you know?"

"That, um, I want to be with you." Her gaze skitters away. She fiddles with my fingers. "That I would regret it for the rest of my life if I didn't try, because... we have something between us I haven't had with anyone else in a very long time and I can't let the teeny tiny fact that I've never been in love with a woman stand in the way now, can I?" She chuckles nervously. "Honestly, Ida, I have no idea what I'm doing. I'm purely going on instinct here, on my gut." She taps against her belly again. "And all my gut has to say is, *Ida, Ida, Ida...*"

I have to laugh a little at how she expresses herself, although I have nothing but admiration for someone doing what they want, simply going for it, like Faye has just done —because it's the opposite of what I've done all my life.

"Really?" I nod at her belly. "If I were to put my ear against your stomach, that's what I would hear? My own name on repeat?"

"Undoubtedly." She brings my hand to her lips and kisses my knuckle. "But, um, us being actors and all that, I do hope you won't hold it against me that I stole your thunder out there."

"You can steal way more than my thunder." I bring our joined hands to my lips and kiss one of her fingertips. "Wrapping this movie was so bittersweet, because I would be seeing much less of you, which is what my head knew I needed, but my heart hadn't fully caught up yet, as usual."

"You'll be seeing much more of me." Faye gives my hand a squeeze.

"Maybe they'll ask us to reshoot both kissing scenes now that they know about us..."

"Some of the crew will at least be having a few light bulb moments."

"What about Leslie, though?" I hate to be a downer, but I'm the woman who stayed in the closet for decades for the sake of my career, while Faye has so recklessly decided to forego the smallest peek into the inside of any closet.

"Leslie works for me," Faye says matter-of-factly.

"You know what I mean. You know what Leslie stands for."

"Sure, but, Ida, over the course of the past few months, I've noticed this change in you. I've seen you gain confidence. I've seen the real you and, look at me now, I'm driving home with you because the real you is so captivating. So impossible to ignore. I need to be with you and I can't do that if I'm going to hide. Not when you're finally telling the world who you really are. That's not an option for me."

"I would never advise you to go in the closet. I've spent enough time in there for both of us." It's easy enough, in the back of this car, pretending that it's just the two of us against the rest of the world, that there won't be any repercussions to what Faye has just done—to her doing in one moment, what it took me decades to gather the courage for.

"Ida," she whispers. "We have the rest of our lives to talk about this." Her head's already slanted in my direction. "Right now, the only thing I think we should be doing is kiss some more."

I can only agree. I meet her halfway, look into those gorgeous eyes of hers, before opening my lips to her again and again.

CHAPTER THIRTY-ONE
FAYE

Ida's teasing me mercilessly. Or maybe she can't believe this is happening. Maybe she needs to take her sweet time with me in order to truly be sure it's really me squirming underneath her fingertips. I can hardly blame her for any of that. I didn't know I was going to do what I did until I did it. Until I walked up to Ida, in all her beguiling glory, and kissed her in front of the entire *A New Day* cast and crew. Because I couldn't not do it. I could hardly stand by and do nothing. It simply wasn't an option.

Ida traces her finger around my nipple again. Her breath is hot in my ear. Her knee rests heavy on my leg, pushing it into the mattress, exposing all of me to the air. My body is a playground for her touch, for one of her relentless fingers roaming across it so excruciatingly slowly, tensing up my muscles, amping up my arousal with every inch it gains on my skin.

Why so slow? I want to ask, but I'm enjoying it too much. This reacquaintance. This version of Ida who is secure enough in everything, in herself and in me, to take her time. We don't need to rush. We're not in Miami anymore. We're in LA, where we live our lives, mostly in private, with small public outbursts when we promote a movie—the promo tour I have coming up should be a lot of fun. But for now, with Ida's divine finger wandering across my skin, I can still pretend my phone and the outside world it represents don't exist. Maybe that's why we're doing this slowly. The longer our reunion lasts, these few hours of seclusion that allow us this unburdened time together, and the longer our climax is postponed, the later we have to face the music.

Ida's finger reaches my belly button. She's barely touching me. Her finger hovers over my skin, yet I can feel it everywhere. I can't blame myself for not knowing that this is what I wanted all along. Because of course I was afraid. Afraid of myself most of all, and what this means for me. Afraid for Ida, because of what this might mean for her. Afraid to never see things clearly again, until I did, when Ida took the mic, and it couldn't be clearer. The possibility of regret seems far away now, because it's the last thing I feel when her lips press against the sensitive skin of my neck and her finger dips lower to draw a circle on my inner thigh.

My breath becomes more ragged, my flesh is on fire for her. Turns out Ida's finger is a powerful weapon of arousal. The way she plays me with it like I'm an instrument she mastered long ago, even though my body is as new to her as hers is to me. The softness of her breast pressed against my side. The hardness of her nipple. The way her knee lies on top of my leg so possessively. The way she's got me under her spell right now, as though all of this was carefully planned, while the truth is it might very well never have happened. Yet me lying here, gasping under her touch, feels wholly inevitable.

Her finger draws closer to the apex of my thighs. It skates ever so gently over my sex, coaxing a deep groan from my throat. Her lips stretch into a smile against my neck. She knows she's got me exactly where she wants me.

I turn my head and face her. Not to beg her to go faster but just to look at her, to look into her beautiful brown eyes and feel that rush of knowing course through me again. The same sensation that surged through me as she came out to everyone. Because I was the only one in that room who knew what a huge moment that was for her.

She sends me a smile. Not the big Ida Burton one but a small, intimate smile, only for me. I respond in kind and just as her fingertip skims along the edge of my clit, she kisses me on the lips with such tenderness, with so much feeling. Our tongues meet in a soft caress and now it's Ida groaning into my mouth, it's Ida who's losing control, and I could take advantage of this moment and flip her onto her back and taste her the way I've been wanting to do since that last night in Miami, but I know I need to give her this. This slow acquisition of my body. The time to express her need for this, for me.

Her finger drifts lower again, softly along my lips at first. Then, Ida breathes more heavily and, soon, to my great relief, her finger slides inside of me, and it feels like I've already gotten everything I wanted. Like Ida's already given me all of her, while it's only the exploratory tip of her finger. Like this is our first time all over again.

Maybe I should have known the first time she did this to me, the first time she took me to this dizzying height of arousal. Maybe it should have been a dead giveaway because of how she made me feel all along. But I'm here now, as her finger slips farther into me, as she claims a little more of me. As she grows bolder and thrusts deeper. As she gazes into my eyes and gives me all this pleasure. All this devotion. All her attention, all her gloriousness focused in the increasing thrust of her finger, all her lust for me burning in her gaze. It's more than enough to tip me over the edge of my own desire and let me freefall through a wonderland of utter satisfaction.

When you know, you know. And there's no doubt left in my mind.

CHAPTER THIRTY-TWO
IDA

"Do you know that Isabel Adler song, 'Somewhere I've never been'?" I ask Faye.

Her naked body is pushed against mine, her arm slung over me as though she has zero intention of ever letting go again. Or maybe she just wants it to be fully occupied at all times so she can't use it to check her phone. I'm surprised Leslie hasn't turned up yet, knocking down my door—or maybe she's doing exactly that to Faye's door right now, but Faye's a long way from home.

"Hm," Faye hums. "Of course, I do."

"The first time she sings the chorus, it's very restrained, with hardly any power behind the notes. The second time, she gives it a bit more and you can feel that it's coming, but we're not there yet, until she goes to town on that chorus like there's no tomorrow the third time around. All that she has is in that final chorus and it finally sounds the way you think it should have sounded all along."

"Are you coming up with some sort of convoluted

metaphor for why you teased me so mercilessly earlier?" Faye pushes herself up and looks at me.

When I see her face, I can't help but smile. I'm so smitten with her, but I haven't found the words yet to express how I feel. Right now, we can only use our bodies, our lips, our hands. Words will come later. Maybe I should have thought of that before I tried to say what I'm trying to say.

"No," I say, half-giggling, unable to control this giddiness inside me. "I was trying to say something deeply meaningful, but your mind's clearly on one thing and one thing only."

Faye nods. "That's right." Her hand reaches for my nipple, but I swat it away.

"Fine. I won't share my hard-won wisdom with you then." I mock-pout.

"Oh, come on, Ida. I crave your wisdom. I need it like, uh, I can't think of anything right now." She sits up a bit straighter. "Sorry. Tell me. I'm all ears."

I take her hands in mine. "For the longest time, I've felt stuck inside the first, very restrained chorus. I always knew there was more to feel, to experience, to… love. But I didn't let myself. Then, I met you and our time in Miami felt like the second, amped-up chorus. Like I was on the edge of something big. Something important. But I wasn't quite there yet. Until now. Now I'm smack dab in the middle of the big finale and I feel it all. I feel everything. I feel all the glory of letting go, of no longer trying to control everything, of just being who I am and allowing it to wash over me. It's…" Words fail me for an instant.

"Ecstatic," Faye whispers. "Sublime."

"Like going from a black-and-white world to lukewarm

sepia to finally, at the cusp of fifty, seeing everything in Ultra HD color for the first time."

"It's an honor to enter this technicolor world with you." She leans in and kisses me gently on the cheek.

"You have no idea how good it is to have you here." Having Faye by my side for all of this is much more than a bonus, it's more than the cherry on top of my coming out cake.

"You gave me a pretty good idea just now." Her smile morphs into a wicked grin. "Now allow me to let you experience the full glory of the final chorus once again." Faye kisses me on the lips this time. "I want you," she says, when we break, and she's already a little breathless again—breathless for me. "I need to taste you."

Who am I to question Faye's needs today? She needed to kiss me in front of everyone a few hours ago and I was more than fine with that. To have Faye walk up to me, to have her take my hands in hers, to have her kiss me like that, to lift the moment into one of sheer perfection, is the greatest thing that has ever happened to me—and it only happened because I revealed my true self to the world.

"I'm all yours," I say in a ragged whisper. I feel myself go wet like a river for her at the anticipation of what she's about to do. At the sight I'm about to witness again. Of Faye's head bowing between my legs, giving me the ultimate pleasure.

Then, she's all over me, pushing me down, her touch hungry, her kisses needy and insistent. And I let her have me, take me, claim me as hers. Because that's what I am, in this bed after the day I've had. I'm all Faye's.

Her tongue is everything when it touches down between my legs. It's hot and soft and oh-so deft and I can't help but think about the very first time she did this, when everything was different. When I wanted her to do this very thing so much, but I wasn't sure that she would. But she did so anyway, without trepidation, leaving me to wonder, in the haze of my arousal, why I got to be so lucky. Now, I wonder again. Because I am lucky and I'm happy and I no longer care what anyone else thinks about that. I've cared for way too long. I was stuck in a loop of my own making in the first chorus. A loop I found impossible to break. A destructive loop that made me give up the very thing Faye is doing to me right now—and so much more.

"Oh, Faye," I whisper, as I surrender to my desire. As I give myself what I've craved for years and years. As I succumb to Faye's touch and all it stands for. As I do what I should have done all my life.

CHAPTER THIRTY-THREE
FAYE

For weeks, my life has been a madhouse, because of course someone shared a video of me kissing Ida and of course it went viral. The only respite I find is in Ida's arms, which is ironic, because the desire to be in Ida's arms is what created this media frenzy about us in the first place.

I'm happy to deflect some of the more probing questions away from Ida and her coming out, her marriage to Derek, women she's been with including those who have decided to ignore the nondisclosure agreements they signed at the time in return for their own fifteen minutes of fame. I take it all gladly because, in the end, I get to be with Ida. I get to drive to her place, run the gauntlet of the paps, park my car behind the gate, and wrap my arms around her. And it's all worth it. The media frenzy will die down in the end, but what Ida and I have, hopefully, will only grow stronger.

"I'll go with you to Europe," she said this morning, when I had to ask her to, quite literally, push me out of bed. "I don't want you to have to do any of this on your own." But I was already late for the press junket I find myself at now, bombarded with question after question about Ida, and, to the director and producer's understandable dismay, not about the movie I'm supposed to promote.

"Any buzz will be good for this movie," Leslie told them earlier. "I've worked in this town long enough to know what gets asses in seats. Don't worry about it." But of course the director is worried because he wants to discuss his movie, not one of his actors' sudden shift in sexual preference—especially because in this movie my character has to choose between two guys.

Most actors hate days like this where they have to reply to the same question again and again. It's not my favorite activity in the world—especially not now when I have Ida in my life—but I pride myself on my professionalism when it comes to promotional activities. No matter how tedious, I will always make the most of it because it's an inherent part of the job. It's all part of the big Hollywood game.

Max, the PR person for this event, has had a desperate slant to his head all day, and I feel guilty, because it was never my intention to hijack this junket, nor to jeopardize the chances of this movie at the box office. This movie was the very last thing on my mind when I stepped up to kiss Ida, because I'm more than just an actor. In that moment, I just wanted Ida. I wanted to show her how much I could be there for her, how proud I was of her, how much I admired her for her courageous revelation.

Today, I'm paying the price.

Max points at a journalist in the seats in front of us.

"A question for Faye," the woman says.

Next to me, I can hear my two male co-stars sigh for the umpteenth time today. I try to give the woman my full attention.

"Given recent revelations about you and Ida Burton, do you think the audience will still find you believable in this movie as Tessa, the woman who has to fall for those two hunks sitting next to you?"

Danny White audibly groans next to me. Mario Velez, my other co-star, seems to have morphed into a statue, like he's given up on the whole thing even though we have a few more hours of this to go today, and a few more weeks after that until the movie premieres.

I can't be snippy. I can't be snarky. I have to be polite and witty and eloquent, because that's the deal when you're on this side of the table as far as I'm concerned. But I'm also at my wit's end, because I've made all the lame jokes already. I've responded to a question in this vein a dozen times before. Yet, the journalists keep trying, keep pressing me for something inadvertent, something I might regret saying later, something that will yield them excellent clickbait for their outlet.

"Okay, look..." I keep my voice so friendly it's almost saccharine. "I'm very sorry, but I'm not going to be responding to any more questions about Ida and me. She has nothing to do with this movie." I cast my glance at the press corps opposite me. They're only doing their job, of course, and it's a hell of a lot harder than mine. If I give them a little something, I may be able to redirect their attention back to this movie. "You can ask Ida and me all you want about us when *A New Day* comes out. I promise you here and now, we'll go above and beyond to answer all of your questions. But right now, I will only answer questions about this wonderful movie Mario, Danny and I are in."

I focus on the woman who asked the last question. "I will

say this, though. Questions like yours are what stand in the way of giving the audience at least a chance to believe my character. When you truly think about it, what would stop them from believing me? Because that's just how it is? Well, that's no longer an excuse for anything. The status quo is over and done with. As for myself, good heavens yes, I'm a different person now that I'm with Ida."

I can feel the agitation in the room grow. I hadn't meant to launch into an impromptu speech, but I can hardly back down now. "But that doesn't make this movie any different. Because it doesn't matter who I love. Does it matter who Danny loves? Who Mario's with? When you go to the theater and you want to have a good time? When you want a movie to put a smile on your face? I believe in this movie a hundred percent and I'm so absolutely certain it will put that smile on your face and the fact that I've gone and fallen in love with Ida Burton has nothing to do with that.

"In the end, I'm just a woman, same as you, a human, same as anyone else in this room. I'm sure that I'm not the only one in this room to have fallen for another woman later in life—or a man for a man." Always a much safer bet when dealing with a bunch of movie reporters. "As I'm also sure that you know the answer to your own question very well." I can't help but pin my gaze on the reporter who asked the question again. "Of course, the audience will believe me. This is what I do. Acting is my calling. My life's work. I've been doing it for decades. Why would movie-goers suddenly stop believing what I do now just because I've fallen in love with someone unexpected?"

The woman doesn't seem to have any follow-up questions. The room is eerily quiet for long seconds. Next to me, Danny perks up, straightens his spine. On my other side,

Mario holds up his hand, effectively shutting up a journalist who is starting to say something.

"Give Faye a round of applause, please." Mario stands up, looks at me, and starts clapping. "For saying some things that needed to be said."

The applause starts slowly but as soon as Danny rises from his seat as well and starts applauding me—making me feel very self-conscious in the process, despite being used to this, although not *quite* this—the room acquiesces.

Change is always slow and always starts small, Ida said the other day, but every little push forward helps. I can only hope this has helped the teensiest bit.

During the break that follows, I text Ida to say yes to her going overseas with me. Not only because I don't want to be away from her for a few weeks. We have some points to prove and everything is easier with Ida by my side.

CHAPTER THIRTY-FOUR
IDA

"If no one ever defies the audience's expectations, how can their expectations ever get a chance to change?" Charlie says. "It's a chicken-and-egg situation, if you ask me."

Ava and Charlie have invited Faye and me to dinner, and to just simply sit here with another couple made up of two women, with Faye next to me, is a treat in itself. It doesn't hurt that we're looking out over the ocean and that I have the prospect of waking up to the same view, in Faye's bed, tomorrow morning.

"It will change, over time," Faye says. "If more actors do what Ida has done."

"And what Faye has done," Ava says. "For which I would like to get some credit where credit's due, please." I see how she winks at Faye.

"Babe." Faye turns to me. "Just so you know, if it weren't for Ava, we wouldn't be sitting here together right now." Her smile is dazzling and a little playful. "We simply owe her *everything*."

I can't help myself. And I don't have to. Without qualms, I close the distance between us and kiss Faye full on the lips.

"Oh my god," Charlie groans. "If only I'd known about this when we started shooting."

"This…" Faye waves her hand about. "Wasn't going on when we started shooting. Ida was still locked in her closet and I had no idea she was going to seduce me like that."

Charlie pokes Ava in the elbow. "You may claim all the credit, babe, but it's the movie Liz and I wrote that started all of this."

"I can't really argue with that." Ava blows Charlie a kiss.

"Excuse me, but I didn't seduce you," I say. "If anything, it was the other way around."

How things have changed, I think, as I enjoy the easy banter between the four of us. What an utter triumph to sit here, feeling so free and unencumbered.

" To think Ava wanted to cast herself in your part, Ida," Charlie says, while ducking away from her wife.

"I've made peace with that now." Ava grabs Charlie by the back of the neck and pretends to shake her about. "If I'd made you give me Ida's part, as I said, we wouldn't be sitting here right now."

"Made me?" Charlie draws up her eyebrows. "How were you ever going to make me do that?"

Ava cocks her head and fixes Charlie with a stare. "We both know I can make you do anything I want. If anything, it's too easy for me; you're putty in my hands."

I chuckle and glance at Faye, wondering if we will ever reach this comfortable but delicious stage together. If all of this is in the cards for us, too. I sure hope so. I smile at her, because that's just the way my lips go when I lay eyes on her, and kiss her, again, just because I can.

The other day, we hiked all the way up to the Hollywood sign, just so that I could kiss her there, above that iconic landmark, in this town that has made me who I am. And maybe it was all worth it. Maybe it wasn't a mistake for me to stay sequestered in my golden closet for so long, because I was also waiting for Faye.

"Seriously, though," Charlie says and raises her glass. "To Ida and Faye. What you're doing right now is still so important. We may find it a bit ridiculous how much movie stars are looked up to because it holds them to impossible standards. Hell, it kept Ida in the closet for way too long. But for you two to be out like this is such a major thing."

"You're just saying that because it will make your movie a guaranteed box office hit." It's easy enough to tell Ava is actually proud of Charlie, she just can't help needling her.

"Absolutely not," Charlie says. "There are no guarantees at the box office. None. Zero. This is still super risky in so many ways."

"To this movie, then." Faye lifts her glass as well. "To everything that made it possible for *A New Day* to be made. To Charlie and Liz for writing it. To Ida for taking the part of Veronica—and finding the courage to seduce *me*."

"I think you knew all along how irresistible you were." Turns out, I love needling Faye too. "You invited me over for kissing practice, remember?"

"Only because you were falling apart in rehearsals. I thought you were scared of kissing another woman while all you wanted was to ravage me." Turns out, Faye's not beyond it either—although there's also a lot of truth in what she's saying.

Later, when Faye and I walk home along the beach, we stop before heading inside, our feet in the sand, the sound of the surf in our ears.

I pull Faye close to me, inhale her scent, and she buries her nose in my hair.

"Sometimes, I think you have more of a crush on my hair than on me," I whisper in her ear.

"I do love your hair," Faye says. "Keep it this way for a while just to be on the safe side." I can feel her body convulse against mine as she snickers. "Do you want to walk for a bit?"

I nod and take her hand in mine as we walk along the beach, the moon overhead, my heart jumping with joy.

"I've been meaning to ask." Faye pulls me a little closer. "In Miami, you told me it had been two years and four months since you'd slept with another woman."

"Hm." An image of Martha pops up in my head. It doesn't hurt any longer to think of her.

"Care to give me a few more details about this mysterious and very lucky woman who got to share Ida Burton's bed?"

"Believe me, she wasn't lucky in the long run." I take a deep breath, and start. "She was a producer on a movie I did a while ago."

"Which one?" Faye wants all the details then. Maybe she wants to google her. It's an understandable reflex. I've looked up Brian Walsh and know much more about him than I did before.

"*Only You Will Do*," I say. "Martha's gaze lingered, you know? And I couldn't look away. Sometimes, I just couldn't, despite my best intentions."

"Oh, I know." Faye bumps her shoulder into mine.

"Pretty quickly, we started chatting about more than the movie and there was this charge in the air when I stood close to her. One thing led to another and…"

"And?" Faye curls her arm around my waist and pulls me close.

"We had a very secret affair, which made me so paranoid, it was doomed from the start."

"You weren't ready to come out yet?"

I shrug. "I guess not."

"Have you had many secret affairs like that?" We stop. We should start making our way back to her house soon.

"I wouldn't say many. A few. Three or four, I guess, over the years. They all ended badly, because… I couldn't accept myself. That's what it boils down to in the end. I didn't respect myself enough to accept this crucial part of me…" I look into the mid-distance. I can never turn back the clock and give myself back the time before I came out, but I have this now. I'm standing here with Faye and it might not make up for everything, but it makes up for a lot.

"Hey, I've had to do some soul-searching as well, what with suddenly being so interested in the ladies and all that…"

Faye never fails to put a smile on my face. Never. It's dark around us and she probably can't see how she's just made me smile again but she doesn't need to see to know.

"I've had to look deep inside myself and I can no longer just accept things for what they are the way I once did. But I've learned this…" She pulls me closer. "You have the most magical hair, for starters." We burst into a silly giggle again —we've been doing a lot of that since she kissed me at the wrap party. "Everything changes all the time. So do we. I'm not the same woman I was when I was with Brian. As the woman I was before we made this movie together. And neither are you, Ida. But please don't sell yourself short for the choices you made, because the fact that you made them when you did means you had a good reason at the time. But times have changed and so have those reasons. And here we are."

"Beautiful *and* wise—"

"Beyond my years," Faye is quick to say.

"I disagree." I look into her eyes which are the same color as the ocean this time of night. "I had to turn fifty to know all of this."

Faye nods. "I hope it was worth the wait."

In response, I can only kiss her with all I have in me.

CHAPTER THIRTY-FIVE
FAYE

"Here we go," Ida says, and takes my hand in hers. No one has asked us to walk onto the red carpet like this, but we wouldn't have it any other way. I want Ida's hand in mine. I want nothing more than to be photographed next to her.

I give her a quick nod. It's been nearly eight months since I kissed Ida at the wrap party of the very movie that's premiering today—the movie that changed our lives. We've been out in public many times, but this is the first time we're walking onto a red carpet together. The press line is thick. The buzz is frenetic. Everyone wants a shot of us, despite the fact that Ida and I being together is no longer news. Yet, when we step out like this, especially to promote the movie that made it all happen, everyone wants a piece of the action.

I'm no different. I want to soak up every last ounce of this unique experience. After all, Ida and I may never do a movie together again. But even if we do, it will never again be the first one we did together—nor will it be the one where we fell in love.

"Ida. Faye. Ida. Faye." It's like the chorus of a song that someone's performing especially for us. The photographers' flashes create a strobe light effect.

Ida and I pose, our hands firmly clasped together. I'm not letting go of her. I've held onto her for months now. Months during which nothing's been overly difficult, nor has it been overly easy either. I've introduced Ida to flabbergasted friends and family and learned that, in these circumstances, it does really help that you've fallen for one the biggest movie stars in the world. Even my brother showed a deference I never knew he possessed.

I've had to face questions I didn't know the answer to. Questions from myself most of all. But after all this time, I'm still so smitten with Ida, still so utterly convinced we have a beautiful future together, that it wasn't all that hard after all. It's just my life now. My life with Ida. And Ida makes everything better.

We're standing in the middle of the red carpet. In the midst of this roar of flashing lights with questions being hurled at us, and I remember the promise I made when I was promoting my previous movie. I told the press they could ask Ida and me anything they wanted when *A New Day* came out. When I told Ida she gave me one of her hearty laughs and shook her head, but, tonight, we do have a plan.

"Ready?" she asks.

I nod, again, then turn to her, and kiss her fully on the lips. And I can't help myself. I open my mouth a little. Let the tip of my tongue meet hers. Then we break into a smile, because doing this with Ida makes me smile more than anything.

"Naughty," she whispers, and I go weak in the knees as I always do.

Before we came here, we figured we might as well give the press exactly what they wanted. They may think they want to know the very last detail of our private life more than anything, but a picture says so much more than all the words we can ever speak. The picture of Ida and me kissing on the red carpet will travel all around the world at record speed, spreading various messages depending on who's looking at it.

To the teenage girl wondering about her sexual preference, it will say that it's okay to be gay and it's okay to doubt. To the woman deeply in the closet, it will say that she can take all the time she needs—because look at Ida. To most, it will just be a passing image of two people kissing. Some might not even bat an eyelid that it's two women. Some won't have a clue of who we are. Some will print it out and hang it on their wall to be reminded of it when they need some extra strength, or just a little nudge to make it through a rough day.

In the end, all Ida and I want to say with this profusely photographed kiss is that it's perfectly normal. It's perfectly okay. There's not one little thing wrong with it. It's not a stunt, even though we know it will get the media purring like a kitten. Because our love is real. The kiss is real. We are real women with real lives and real feelings and we have chosen each other. I choose Ida every day. She chooses me. That's what we want to say. Our radical openness can't eradicate all prejudice and hate and homophobia, but it's a damn good place to start.

Ida and I break apart to answer a few quick questions about the movie and, inevitably, our relationship. Because of our status, we were the last to walk the red carpet, and we're asked to go into the theater for the screening. We've seen the movie already last week at a private event for the cast and crew. We might be biased, but we both loved it.

The producer gives a short speech, followed by Tamara saying a few words, then the theater goes dark. I sink into my seat, Ida's hand in my lap, and look forward to reliving the beginning of our love story once again.

EPILOGUE
FIVE YEARS LATER

I blink into the bright sunlight to find Faye on the deck, overlooking the ocean.

"She finally rises." Faye holds her arms open for me. "Come here."

I walk over to her. "I'm getting too old for night shoots." I look over the deck's railing. "Where are the LBFs?" It's how we refer to our children sometimes, short for Leesa and Leroy Burton-Fleming.

"Next door. I'll call Ava to ask if they're not being too much of a nuisance."

"What does it say about us as mothers that our children prefer to spend their Saturday with the lesbians next door?" I lean into Faye.

"That they are very considerate and well-educated kids who want to give us some much-needed alone time." Faye taps her wrist. "I was about to come wake you in the most irresistible fashion."

"In that case, I'm going back to bed. Just pretend I never

came out here." My attention is drawn to two figures on the beach, sprinting toward the ocean.

"There's Leesa. She said something about teaching Charlie how to surf."

"Poor Charlie. Do you think our daughter has a crush on her?"

Faye turns to me. "She's only eleven."

"Only?" I start to say, but Faye's cell starts buzzing in her pocket. She fishes it out.

"It's Ava." Faye shoots me a knowing glance. "Do send them home," she says as soon as she picks up. "Although you should never have gotten that puppy. Leroy can't shut up about it. I bet he's all over it right now."

I watch Faye as she talks on the phone with Ava. Motherhood looks good on her. The way she strokes Leroy's hair when we're lounging in front of the TV in the evening. How she patiently explains to Leesa, over and over again, that there's a time for surfing and a time for homework, without ever raising her voice.

Even though our house is full of life and frantic energy at times, a calmness has come over Faye since we brought Leroy and Leesa home three years ago. Like she finally is exactly where she belongs. Like she's finally fully come home. Kind of like how I felt when I arrived home deep in the night to a quiet, dark house where everyone was sleeping and I had to tip-toe around so as not to wake my wife or children. Even though I've been married before—Derek is Leesa's doting godfather—it was never even remotely like that in my previous marriage.

Faye ends the call and beams me a wide smile. "Ava's making some sort of elaborate Mexican dish with Leroy. The kids are staying for lunch. She invited us, but…"

"You have other plans?" I let my robe drop down my shoulders a fraction. "Because I'm quite hungry."

"Hunger," Faye says, as she takes a step closer to me, "I can definitely work with." She can't drag me inside the house fast enough, up the stairs, past the poster of *A New Day* we had framed and hung in a spot we walk by numerous times every single day.

No one could have dreamed up how big a hit that movie would be. How big a smile it would put on people's faces. How they would want to witness, again and again, how Mindy and Veronica fell in love. How Faye and I kissed for the very first time, for the camera, but, ultimately, also very much for us.

How it would relaunch my career. How times had changed already but we didn't know, or we did, at least Faye and I did, because, for us, everything had changed already.

I eagerly follow Faye up the stairs I just walked down. We tumble into our bedroom. She pushes my robe off me and, in a gesture so familiar, so comforting, so inextricably Faye, slides her hands into my hair.

"I love you, Ida Burton-Fleming," she whispers in my ear as we land on the unmade bed.

"Not as much as I love you, Faye Burton-Fleming," I reply, as I always do.

Faye takes a moment to look at me, to really gaze down at me, the way she sometimes does, as though she still needs to take a moment to drink it all in. All that has happened. All that we've become. Only then can she kiss me, as though she hasn't kissed me a million times before already.

GET THREE E-BOOKS FOR FREE

Building a relationship with my readers is the very best thing about writing. I occasionally send newsletters with details on new releases, special offers and giveaways.

And if you sign up to my mailing list I'll send you all this free stuff:

1. An e-book of *Few Hearts Survive*, a Pink Bean Series novella that is ONLY available to my mailing list subscribers.
2. A free e-book of *Hired Help*, my very first (and therefore very special to me) lesbian erotic romance story.
3. A free e-book of my first 'longer' work, my highly romantic novella *Summer's End*, set on an exotic beach in Thailand.

You can get *Few Hearts Survive* (a Pink Bean Series novella), *Hired Help* (a spicy F/F novelette) and *Summer's End* (a deeply romantic lesfic novella) **for free** by signing up at www.harperbliss.com/freebook/ or scanning the QR code below

ABOUT THE AUTHOR

Harper Bliss is a best-selling lesbian romance author. Among her most-loved books are the highly dramatic French Kissing and the often thought-provoking Pink Bean series.

Harper lived in Hong Kong for seven years, travelled the world for a bit, and has now settled in Brussels (Belgium) with her wife and photogenic cat, Dolly Purrton.

Together with her wife, she hosts a weekly podcast called Harper Bliss & Her Mrs.

Harper loves hearing from readers and you can reach her at the email address below.

www.harperbliss.com
harper@harperbliss.com

Made in the USA
Monee, IL
14 April 2024

56960426R00163